by Stanton Forbes

WELCOME, MY DEAR, TO BELFRY HOUSE
BUT I WOULDN'T WANT TO DIE THERE
ALL FOR ONE AND ONE FOR DEATH
THE SAD, SUDDEN DEATH OF MY FAIR LADY
IF LAUREL SHOT HARDY THE WORLD WOULD END
SHE WAS ONLY THE SHERIFF'S DAUGHTER
THE NAME'S DEATH, REMEMBER ME?
GO TO THY DEATHBED
IF TWO OF THEM ARE DEAD
ENCOUNTER DARKNESS
A BUSINESS OF BODIES
TERROR TOUCHES ME
RELATIVE TO DEATH
TERRORS OF THE EARTH
GRIEVE FOR THE PAST

Welcome, My Dear, to Belfry House

Welcome, My Dear, to Belfry House

STANTON FORBES

PUBLISHED FOR THE CRIME CLUB BY
DOUBLEDAY & COMPANY, INC.
GARDEN CITY, NEW YORK
1973

All characters in this book are fictitious, and any resemblance to actual persons, living or dead, is purely coincidental.

Lyrics from THE IRISH BALLAD by Tom Lehrer, copyright © 1952 by Tom Lehrer. Used by permission.

Lyrics from WHEN YOU WORE A TULIP AND I WORE A BIG RED ROSE, words by Jack Mahoney; music by Percy Wenrich, Copyright 1914, Renewed 1942 by Leo Feist Inc. Used by permission.

Book used for research: *The World of Bats* with photographs by Nina Leen and text by Alvin Novick. Published by Holt, Rinehart, Winston, © 1969

ISBN: 0-385-02734-6
LIBRARY OF CONGRESS CATALOG CARD NUMBER: 72–89821
COPYRIGHT © 1973 BY DELORIS FORBES
ALL RIGHTS RESERVED
PRINTED IN THE UNITED STATES OF AMERICA
FIRST EDITION

Somebody said, "We're all bats, the whole world,
*   you know that?"*
Wonder what he meant.

Desmodus Rotundus, *the*
common vampire bat. When
early European naturalists
discovered blood-drinking bats,
they named them vampires
because of old legends telling
of creatures that roamed in the
night feeding on human blood.

*Welcome, My Dear,
to Belfry House*

Rousettus Aegyptiacus, *the dog-faced bat has large, protuberant eyes with a well-developed iris. The Rousettus are the only Megachiroptera to orient acoustically. They are really a rather pretty bat with a reddish brown furry face like a tiny terrier.*

Cheryl . . .

She got up, slowly, her knees ached, she wasn't used to praying, she wasn't very good at it. Lack of practice. She tried to recall when she'd last done it, memory flickered, a small girl in a blue night suit, one with feet in it, but the film faded and left like a test pattern on a TV screen, became a picture of Mother in her coffin.

Mother. Oh, Mother! If I could only be with you in that dark hole.

"Miss Harris? Cheryl?"

She took a deep breath. Another. "Yes?"

"It's Ralph Clawson, Miss Harris. May I come in?"

She'd locked the study door, she'd forgotten that she'd done that for privacy. Martha must have let him in. She'd forgotten, also, that she had an appointment with Ralph Clawson at three o'clock and her watch told her it was five minutes past the hour. "Of course," she said brightly, too loudly, "come in." And went to open the door for him. The

3

time, the slow, slow time, so perverse, slipping by when it shouldn't, dragging its minutes when it should hurry.

Ralph Clawson stood in the doorway, like God? No, no, God wouldn't look like Mr. Clawson, wearing a dark blue suit with a vest and holding a briefcase in his hand.

"How are you feeling, Miss Harris?" asked God; no, no, asked Mr. Clawson.

"I'm all right. Won't you come in? I thought this would be the room for will reading. Because it has a desk."

Did he look at her strangely? No matter. He came in and went to the desk, put the briefcase down on top of it, remained standing. Why was he standing? Of course, he was waiting for her to sit down. Perfectly obvious, except that her mind wasn't functioning too well. She chose a chair, not the rose chair, that had been Mother's favorite, but a plain side chair without arms, a straight no-nonsense chair that would force her to sit upright and keep level eyes. She moved it closer and sat in it and then Mr. Clawson sat, too, behind the desk.

He opened the briefcase. Click, click went its snap locks. "It's a very nice day outside," he said, removing papers from the briefcase.

"What?" Why in the world would he say that? Flustered, she glanced toward the windows. The sun was shining. "Oh, yes. Yes, it is."

"Have you been out today?" He was arranging things now, a neat stack with a blue-bound document on the top.

"Today?" Had she? She didn't think so. "No, I don't think so."

"Or yesterday?" He removed an eyeglass case from his pocket, took the glasses out of it. So typical of a lawyer, she thought, a proper place for everything. Careful, she warned herself. Your mind is making much of nothing.

"Yesterday? Oh, I must have been out yesterday." She honestly couldn't remember. How long had it been since she'd found Mother cold in her bed? How long since she'd seen her beautified in a copper case?

"You really shouldn't stay cooped up in this house. A young girl like you, you should get out, see people . . ." His voice trailed off, she thought he looked embarrassed.

"I'm grieving."

"Yes, I know. But it's been a week now and—it isn't good for you. Your housekeeper is worried about you." He peered at her over the glasses. They were half-glasses, half moons. They gave him an unexpected pixie-like look.

"Dear Martha." She gave in to self-pity. "She's all I have in the world."

"Well." He cleared his throat. "We'd better get on with this. It's somewhat complicated . . ." He cleared his throat again, looked down at the top paper, began to read.

The words he read said that I, Alice Harris, being of sound mind, etc., do bequeath all my worldly goods to the person known as Cheryl Harris . . .

"Person known as?" she asked.

"A legal phrase," Clawson interjected, went on. The worldly goods of Alice Harris included the house in which they sat and the furnishings of that house and the land on which the house stood and the money in the bank, $53,429.16, and certain stocks and bonds and on and on and on. She had to control an urge to cry out, "Take it back, I don't want it, I want Mother!"

"Now, it will take some time for this to go through probate," her mother's lawyer told her when he'd finally finished reading the will, "but living expenses can be met . . ."

"Thank you. I'll need to pay Martha and the light bill, things like that. Otherwise, it doesn't matter."

"Yes, well, nonetheless . . ." More throat clearing. Perhaps he had a cold. Or he smoked too much. Did he smoke? She didn't know. He put the top document aside, went to the next. The next wasn't flat, spread out like the others, it

5

was folded up into an envelope and the envelope, which he held out to her now, had the word *Cheryl* written on it. "Mrs. Harris left this in my keeping with the instructions to give it to you in the event of her demise," he explained pompously.

She took the envelope from him. It felt heavy. She was reluctant to open it. Unreasonable! A letter from Mother. Saying that she loved her daughter. That was the reason for the reluctance. She might break down and cry in front of this veritable stranger, a man she'd seen maybe a half-dozen times in her twenty-two years.

He read her mind. "Would you rather read it in private?"

"Yes, please."

"Very well. It's necessary that you read it now, before we continue. Perhaps if I went out into the kitchen, your housekeeper would give me a cup of coffee?"

"I'm sure she would." He was understanding. Not like a stranger, she'd been wrong to think that. He was a friend. A new friend. She smiled gratefully at his back as he left.

The envelope was sealed. Opening it, she got a paper cut on her finger. She put the finger in her mouth and sucked on it. After a minute, she took the finger out of her mouth and used both hands to remove the folded pages. There were several, she opened them out and began to read.

My Dear Cheryl,

I thank you, my dear, for all the years of joy you have given me. I've often wondered what my life would have been like if you were not given to me. Empty, I know. I have loved you as though you were my own daughter.

I can see your face now, those big blue-gray eyes widening as you read that last sentence. Don't be dismayed, my dear Cheryl, because you were not my blood daughter. If you had been, I couldn't have cared for you more than I do. In my opinion, a child belongs to the person who cares for it and for whom it cares. We have cared for each other, haven't we?

If there are tears in those eyes, please don't cry. Read on. You were placed in my care when you were just a little thing. I can still remember the first time I saw you, a tiny little girl in a blue night suit with feet, all huge, blue-gray eyes and no hair at all except for a pale blonde wisp tied up on top with a foolish little blue bow. Your grandmother handed you to me and said, "Alice, I will be forever grateful to the gods that I have a friend like you. Someone I can give my grandchild to, gladly." And I promised her, "I'll love her as my own." "I know you will," she said.

Your own parents were dead, you see. They were Alvin and Leila Sechrest, so your true name is Cheryl Sechrest. Your mother and father were killed in a tragic accident and your grandmother couldn't keep you. This may be hard for you to understand until you realize that your grandmother is Deirdre Dunn and you know who Deirdre Dunn is. Everyone does.

We decided, Deirdre and I, that it would be best for you if you believed I was your mother. We decided you would be better off having roots, having a home, having security without questions, explanations, doubts. Whether we were right is purely academic at this point, the deed has been done. But I told Deirdre that when I died, you must know the truth. And she agreed, saying, "Alice, you're twenty years younger than I am. It will all be water over the dam by the time you go. But be sure and tell Cheryl that her wild and weird grandma loved her too well to bring her up as an actress' child." So, if she is dead before you read this, please understand that this rather unusual arrangement was made for love, for no other reason. Take my word for it.

However, if she is alive, go to her. As I write this, she is living in retirement at a place called Belfry House outside of a town called Truro on Cape Cod in Massachusetts. She will welcome you with open arms, I am sure. She writes me often, is hungry for news of you. She was so proud when you graduated from college this spring. And every time I take pictures of you, I have two sets made and send her one. She says you are a beautiful child and although I know you don't think you are, believe me, your grandmother knows.

You will have money and this house. If you choose, you can live here or sell it and go where you wish. But first of all, before you decide, go to visit your grandmother if she is alive. Whether you elect to stay with her is entirely your prerogative. You need not if you prefer. I know so well that one of the great gifts of this world is independence.

And speaking of independence (I must not preach here, I know), the one way in which I feel I have failed you is that I may have overprotected you. I love you so much, my dear, I never wanted you to fall into the pitfalls that I—and others—have known. And so, I fear that you are a little too dependent on me. I should have, for instance, sent you away to school these last four years but I couldn't bear to, I just couldn't bear it. I must ask you, therefore, to forgive me for that. It is a sin, if sin it is, of love.

I write this now—I don't know why, I've put it off for so many years, somehow I feel my affairs should be in order. At any rate, Ralph Clawson has all your papers, your true birth certificate (I hope you don't mind the fact that I loaned you my name) and he will look after you in all legal matters just as capably as he has looked after my affairs over the years. He is, perhaps, on the austere side but underneath he is kind and absolutely trustworthy.

Oh, my dear, what else can I say to you, to comfort

you? Only that you are wonderful, believe it, and life is an exciting adventure and one fast rule of the game is that eventually, all must part from one another. Wherever I am, as you read this, I love you.

Sincerely,

Your (to all intents and purposes) Mother

The words blurred, she held the pages tight against her chest and wept; the tears creeping into the edges of her tightly closed mouth were salty. She needed a handkerchief but she had no handkerchief, not even a tissue.

But she had a grandmother!

Did she? Was Deirdre Dunn still alive? She must be. The letter was written early this summer and a famous person like that, the papers would have devoted a lot of space to it if she had died. Deirdre Dunn, almost always described in glowing phrases . . . first lady of the theatre, movies, the greatest actress of the twentieth century, always, almost always superlatives. Cheryl herself had seen her so many times on television when they did festivals of her old films. Deirdre Dunn as Catherine the Great, Deirdre Dunn as Mary, Queen of Scots, Deirdre Dunn in plays by O'Neill, Ibsen, Shakespeare, Molière, in adaptations of novels by Hemingway, Faulkner, O'Hara. "Deirdre Dunn dances . . . Deirdre Dunn sings . . . Deirdre Dunn laughs." Deirdre Dunn as Sarah Bernhardt, Deirdre Dunn in a new Hitchcock thriller, Deirdre Dunn in everything!

Deirdre Dunn as Grandmother?

Cheryl sniffled and stood up. A box of Kleenex in the bottom drawer of the desk? Yes. She wiped her eyes, blew her nose. So Deirdre Dunn was her grandmother, so Mother— no, Alice Harris, no relation at all—had lied to her all her life and some old lady in Truro, Massachusetts, hadn't wanted her, probably didn't want her now. She went to the door, stepped out into the hall.

"Mr. Clawson, can you come back, please? I'm ready to hear the rest now. Mr. Clawson . . . ?"

"But how will you get from the airport way out to that place—what's the name of it?" Martha, walking out with Cheryl to the cab, carrying one suitcase, wore a troubled expression.

"I've arranged for a car and chauffeur to take me to Truro," Cheryl told her. It was ironical, she thought, that Martha had so little faith in her ability to cope. The housekeeper treated her like a child, she hadn't realized it until the past few days.

The cabbie got out of the taxi, reached for a suitcase. Cheryl gave him hers, took the larger one from Martha, passed that on.

"But, how long will you be gone?" Martha reminded Cheryl of some character in a Dickens book, she couldn't remember which one, somebody's nurse in a fluted white cap, looking anxious, ready for a wringing of hands. Only, of course, Martha wore no fluted cap, no cap at all on her gray-black hair.

"I don't know, Martha." Cheryl reached for Martha's hands.

"Don't worry, I'll call you. When I get there, I'll call you. I'll keep in touch." Martha's hands clutched at hers. "I promise." She shook Martha's hands reassuringly. "I'll keep in touch."

"We'd better get going, miss," the cab driver told her, "if we're going to make the airport on time."

"Cheryl"—Martha's dark eyes shone—"I've been with you ever since you were little. I don't like this—your mother wouldn't like . . ."

Cheryl interrupted, voice sharp. "This is Alice's idea, Martha, her death wish if you will. Now I'll call you when I get there. Don't worry." She started to get into the cab.

"But, Cheryl . . ."

"Martha, you are not my keeper. Remember that, please. I have no keeper. Not any more. I'm free, Martha. As a bird." And she slid into the back seat of the cab, slammed the door. "Please go," she ordered the driver and sat back, thinking, as free as a bird. Only who cared about a bird?

God, said the Bible. The sparrow. God cared about the sparrow's fall. She didn't know whether to laugh or cry. And the melancholy song began to play in her head, why did you lie to me? Why didn't you want me? Why, why, why did you make my life a movie, a play, a lie, lie, lie?

She got a window seat on the plane, the innermost of three chairs. She sat, looking out, seeing men bringing baggage on a low, flat truck. Her second flight. She'd only gone away once before when her mother—when Alice Harris—took her to Washington, D.C. "It's a beautiful city, full of history."

"Pardon me," said the man who bumped her knee with his small suitcase. He gave her an abashed, humble look through glasses that sat slightly crooked on his head, he seemed to be trying to stuff the case underneath his seat with considerable difficulty.

She nodded and pulled her legs in toward the wall of the plane. The man appeared to be all angles, he was much too tall for one thing, he bumped his head now on the overhead, and terribly thin, he folded himself like a jackknife into the seat next to her. Fumbling for his seat belt, he somehow got hold of hers; she jumped, startled. He apologized, she almost snatched back the left half of her belt and snapped it into place.

"Is this seat taken?" Cheryl couldn't see who spoke from the aisle but the voice was a strange one, a cartoon voice, high-pitched and breathless. A record played at the wrong speed. Cheryl, curious, would have looked to see who spoke but she'd have to crane her neck to see around the man, the creature in the middle seat. And now the squeaky voice was saying, "But of course it's taken, it's my seat, isn't it?" The laugh that followed was a he-he-he.

The man in the middle unbuckled his seat belt, apparently making an attempt at some sort of bumbling gallantry and, in rising, hit his head again. Cheryl, glancing quickly, saw that the woman in the aisle was just as improbable to the eye as to the ear. She was short. Very, very short. Until one saw the face, she might have been a child. A midget. Or a dwarf? What was the difference anyway? The little woman saw her looking, smiled and nodded. Embarrassed, Cheryl nodded back, turned her attention to the window.

"Thank you, thank you very much," the little woman was saying to the man in the middle who was leaning now out into the aisle, seemed to be putting something into the overhead rack. Then there was a great deal of movement while the incongruous pair got seated, fastened belts and settled back. The motors of the plane were switched on and the ship began to move out to the runway. The stewardesses babbled and the captain's voice came over the intercom in some sort of welcoming speech that Cheryl couldn't hear because her seat mates were talking. They talked, too, through the demonstration of oxygen equipment and emergency procedures.

Cheryl shut her eyes and tried to shut her ears as the plane accelerated and left the ground.

"Oh," squealed the little woman in the end seat, "I really don't like flying at all but it's the only practical way to go when you're in a hurry."

"Nothing to worry about," the bumbling man told her. He had a deep voice but his enunciation was poor, somewhat of a mumble. "More accidents on the highways than in the air."

"Yes, I suppose so." Paper rustled. "Will you have a cough drop?"

"No, thanks. Do you mind if I smoke? They've turned off the no smoking sign."

"No, I don't mind. A pipe? How nice. I love the smell of a pipe."

"Do you mind if I smoke?"

Cheryl opened her eyes. It seemed the question was addressed to her. "No." Blessed silence while he packed his pipe with tobacco from a pouch, lit it.

"I'm going to visit a dear friend," the woman on the end said gaily in that peculiar voice. "She said, 'Helena, you come on up here and stay as long as you like.' Now that's what I call a real friend, don't you?"

"Where does your friend live?" He sounded interested, not merely polite. One of those people who struck up lengthy conversations with utter strangers. Mother—Alice Harris—had often told Cheryl, be polite but don't get intimate with people you don't know.

"Outside of Boston. On Cape Cod, actually. She's got this huge house, I've never seen it but I've heard all about it, and she keeps it full of people all the time. She's a wonderful woman."

The man sucked on his smelly pipe. "Sounds as though she never gets lonely."

"Oh, never. But you see, it's more than that. She remembers old friends. That's a rare trait, don't you think? She keeps in touch, busy as she is, and when any of her old friends run into hard luck—sickness or loss of work or just plain down —no matter what the reason, she sends for them and brings them to Belfry House."

Cheryl turned abruptly to look at the speaker. Her mouth was ready to ask, "Belfry House?" but the man put the question for her.

"Yes, that's the name of her house. Funny name, isn't it? But then Deirdre is no ordinary person—I'm sure you know who she is. Deirdre Dunn. The actress."

"Yes," said the man softly. "I know who she is."

"Well, I'm in show business myself, you see, but there's not much of a demand for my kind of work right now and Deirdre found out that I wasn't working"—when she made that funny little face she reminded Cheryl of a monkey—"found out, to tell the truth, that I hadn't been working for some time, so she sent me a check and insisted, 'Helena, you come right up to Belfry House.'"

Should she tell her, Cheryl wondered. Come right out and say, "Deirdre Dunn is my grandmother?" If she did, the woman, Helena whatever her name was, would ask all sorts of questions, questions that Cheryl didn't want to answer.

"She wouldn't answer my letters," said the man to Helena.

"Deirdre? Deirdre wouldn't answer your letters? You mean that you know her, too? But why didn't she answer? That's not like Deirdre."

He shrugged. "I don't really know her, perhaps that's why. My name is Evan Garson, I'm a physiologist, you see, and Miss Dunn's house is, as you say, an unusual one. I asked if I could pay a visit and do some research. I didn't ask to stay at Belfry House, naturally, just to visit. But she wouldn't even acknowledge the fact that I'd written."

"Do some research? I don't even know what a physiologist does. What kind of research?"

"I specialize in experimental work with bats." He spoke as though that explained everything.

This time Cheryl couldn't keep from speaking. "Bats?"

Evan Garson smiled at her around the stem of his pipe. "Yes, bats. I'm writing a book about them, fascinating creatures, and that's why the house is called Belfry House, you see. It provides shelter for a tremendous number of bats, one of the largest colonies outside of some natural caves. A friend of mine stumbled across the information while on vacation up on the Cape last summer, couldn't tell me much about it but if it is as he's heard, it's probably the only house of its sort . . ."

Helena squeaked, "Bats! Ugh!"

Garson sighed gently. "Yes, I know. That's the natural reaction. I understand it, I've felt that nearly universal unreasoning fear myself. But it's important to learn about them. Do you realize that they number in the billions, they're the second largest population of mammals on earth . . . ?"

"Why would Deirdre Dunn live in a house full of bats?" Cheryl interrupted. "Why doesn't she exterminate them?"

He turned back to her, his dark eyes behind the glasses held a dreamy expression even as they sparkled with enthusiasm. "But Miss Dunn wouldn't do that. I understand that she encourages them, provides what is described as a virtual bat sanctuary. I feel certain that she knows as much about bats from a layman's viewpoint as anyone."

"Bats!" Helena's wrinkled little face was horrified. "But I can't live in a house with bats!"

"Now, now." Garson moved as though to pat her shoulder. "I didn't mean to alarm you. As I understand it, they're housed in the top of a tower, they don't fly at large through the residence. They are as timid of people as we are of them, you see, and they have this remarkable built-in sonar . . ."

Cheryl leaned back against her seat. What sort of place was she flying toward? To a woman she didn't know, to a houseful of very odd people if Helena here was an example, with a tower filled with bats. If she could have, she would have gotten off the plane and turned back. Well, she couldn't do that but when she reached Boston she could reverse directions. Could—and would. She suddenly felt cold and a little ill. Could it be that her only living relative was—crazy? Was Belfry House some sort of private madhouse? It would explain the arrangement with Mother, but it wouldn't explain Mother's—Alice's—urge that she visit her grandmother.

"Put your snack table down," Evan Garson was speaking to her, bringing her back to the present.

She looked up. A stewardess stood in the aisle offering her a tray of food. "I'm sorry," Cheryl apologized and pulled down the counter on the seat back in front of her. The food looked appetizing enough but she wasn't sure she was hungry. The Garson man asked the stewardess if she had beer, was told there was none. Cheryl unwrapped her eating utensils, poked at a fruit salad with her fork.

"What is it you do in the theatre, Miss . . . ?" Garson asked Helena while buttering his roll.

"Helena Edwards. I'm a dancer. Did you see *The Wizard of Oz?* The film, that is. Of course, everybody's seen it. I was one of the Munchkins."

"Oh, yes. That Judy Garland, what a wonderful actress she was."

"I was very fond of Judy. Damn' shame what happened. And Bert Lahr gone, too." Helena Edwards sighed deeply, brightened. "But many of my old friends are still alive and kicking. Forrestor McMann, remember him? He's up at Deirdre's and so is Lindsay Ball and the Three Cuckoos . . ."

"The Three Cuckoos? Those comics who used to make all those short subjects, the ones that ran before the main feature?"

Cheryl, listening despite herself, thought she vaguely recalled three men by that silly name, she'd seen them on television as a child. The names Forrestor McMann and Lindsay Ball meant nothing to her. Could Lindsay Ball be related to Lucille Ball?

Evan Garson didn't know them either. He asked who they were and Helena obliged happily. "Forrestor had what we called a special act. He was very well known at one time, but of course you're too young. He got his big break on one of the Major Bowes amateur hours. You may not remember Major Bowes, either, he was before Ted Mack. Anyway, Forrestor plays all sorts of unusual instruments, the spoons, balloons, bicycle pumps, a saw, and his big finale comes when he plays a harmonica with his nose."

Cheryl stared at the little old lady in complete disbelief. Helena caught the glance, laughed merrily. "Yes, I know. It sounds ridiculous but it really is entertaining. He was very big on radio but the years pass and audiences change. Once in a while now he gets a guest shot on a TV variety show, but you can't eat on that so Deirdre took him under her wing and now the old boy hasn't got a care in the world."

"And Lindsay Ball?" prodded Garson. "Who is he?"

"Oh, it isn't a he. It's a she. Lindsay was one of the great beauties in musical comedy. She started with Ziegfeld in one of his *Follies* when she was still a child, did some shows for George White, the *Scandals*, no, I can see that doesn't mean anything to you. She never made a movie, that's why you haven't seen her on television. But she was so lovely and very talented, I can testify to that." She bobbed her little head for emphasis, put a forkful of sliced ham to her birdlike mouth.

"If I may say so, Miss Edwards"—Evan Garson ripped open his sugar bag, managed to spill some of it on Cheryl—"I beg your pardon. If I may say so, Miss Edwards, you surely do not look your age. Florenz Ziegfeld lived such a long time ago. I mean that as a compliment, you understand."

Helena hee-heed. "Somebody said to me the other day, 'Why, you can't be a contemporary of Deirdre Dunn. She must be older than God.' And I said, don't you believe it. You forget that we started very young and worked very hard. Deirdre is in her sixties, that's all. I don't consider that older than God."

Cheryl leaned forward. "What is she like? I mean, what is she *really* like?"

Helena Edwards chewed thoughtfully. "That's kind of hard to put into words," she said when she'd swallowed. "There's really no one to compare her to. She's the one and only Deirdre. I've known her so long, she's become several people. When she was young, determined. Yes, very determined. Perhaps not very likable even. But then, as things came to her, kinder, kinder all the time, terribly considerate. And capable, you simply can't throw her. No matter what the emergency, she's equal to it." She blushed, smiled. "I sound like a one-woman fan club, don't I?"

"She sounds like an extraordinary person," Garson told her. "But in that case, I can't see why she didn't pay me the courtesy of at least answering my letters. I wrote her twice."

"It isn't like her. Maybe she was busy or—are you on your way there now? To see her?"

He nodded, his glasses slipped, they didn't seem to fit very well, he pushed them back on his nose. "That's my plan. I thought the worst that could happen would be that she'd throw me out."

Helena Edwards shook her gray head vigorously. "Not Deirdre, that wouldn't be like Deirdre at all. She'd never turn anyone away from her house. Not Deirdre."

Not even, wondered Cheryl, a long-lost granddaughter that she'd never wanted? She'd changed her mind, she wouldn't turn back after all. She was going to walk up to that house, ring the doorbell and say, "Grandmother. I've come for that present you give so freely. I've come for love. Have you got any left over for me, your own flesh and blood?"

"Jesus!" The driver of the limousine spoke reverently.

"I don't believe it." Helena Edwards's voice climbed to new heights.

"Well, well, well," murmured Evan Garson.

Cheryl, who had decided just prior to landing to offer the pair a ride to Belfry House, was suddenly glad she had. It wasn't the house she'd pictured at all, this incongruous building rising from the dunes. It was a very large house from the looks of it, weather-beaten gray in color and Victorian in architecture. It was almost as though it had been fitted together as a macabre dollhouse for giant dolls, the four stories on the right under one hip roof, then the center part, a shorter connecting piece dominated by a tower five—or was it six—stories high; and then a left section, the twin of the right. A porch grew off the tower, melded the parts together, its balconyed roof upheld by pillars. An elongated house, its tallness accented by long windows set in pairs in intricate frames tied together by curved overhangs that matched the curved upper frames of the windows themselves.

"It reminds me of Oz." Helena suppressed a nervous giggle. "It looks like the Wicked Witch of the West had it flown here." She tittered then. "I wonder if it landed on top of her."

Evan peered out through the car window. "Of course, we won't see any bats at this time of day. They're nesting now, asleep."

"The place looks empty," said Cheryl doubtfully.

"Oh, there'll be people there," Helena assured her. "Drive up to the door, driver."

Cheryl had the impression that he hesitated before putting the limousine in gear and moving closer. The tall windows seemed to be curtained with heavy lace. When the car wheels had ceased scattering the gravel, they could hear from somewhere behind the dunes the hiss of the ocean. A bumblebee flew past the car, found a scraggly rose bush by the side of the porch, buzzed among the half-dozen wild roses blooming there. They could hear him quite clearly, it was that quiet.

Helena Edwards got out of the car, stood on the bottom porch step on stumpy legs and trilled, "Yoo hoo. Anybody home?"

The bumblebee, disturbed and perhaps disappointed, departed.

Cheryl slowly opened her own car door. Helena went up onto the porch, moved out of the sun into the coolness of the porch roof and twisted a knob on the doorjamb. Cheryl could hear the door bell sounding raucously inside.

"Are you sure this is the right place?" she asked the driver.

"It said Belfry House on the mailbox at the turn-off, didn't it?" His tone was something less than polite.

"Perhaps they've gone away." Evan spoke morosely.

Helena rapped vigorously on the screen door frame, called,

"Deirdre! Lindsay! Forrestor! Anybody here? It's me. Helena. Helena Edwards."

"Darling." The voice startled Cheryl, she hadn't heard footsteps but someone stood in the shadowy doorway, someone with long dark hair, wearing some sort of long, light-colored garment.

"Darling!" squealed Helena. The screen door opened and the tall woman inside hugged the small woman. "Who's with you?" asked the wraith, shielding her eyes.

"Come on, come on." Helena gestured to the couple in the car. "Here's Lindsay. It's all right. Somebody's home, after all."

Cheryl stepped out and shut the door, Evan came from his side. The driver got out, too, stood uncertainly. "Get the luggage," Cheryl told him and went up on the porch.

"This is Cheryl Harris," Helena was saying. "She's the daughter of an old friend of Deirdre's and this is Evan Garson, he's a scientist. Studying bats. Are there really bats here, Lindsay?"

Lindsay Ball blinked at them myopically. Her overlong, thin hair clung to her neck and hung over her shoulders. The dress she wore was either a faded yellow or an aged white curled around her body in ruffles. Her eyes were light blue, so light they seemed almost vacant. Her face looked painted on, clownish, carefully drawn eyebrows and mouth and even a little black dot at the side of her mouth. (Didn't they used to call that a beauty mark?) Lindsay Ball's face, Cheryl imagined, was glazed, would crack when she smiled. How old could she be? As old as the dress? Even older?

"Where do you want the bags?" asked the driver, coming up behind them carrying suitcases.

"Bags?" Lindsay Ball blinked again. "Oh, bring them in, I guess. Come in, all of you, it's much too hot. Deirdre's having a massage, it's rest hour, you see, and everybody's napping or

23

reading or whatever . . . come in. The sun is very bad for the complexion."

"There." The driver dropped a duffle bag and Cheryl's small case on the floor with a thud. "I guess that's the lot."

Cheryl counted, her two bags, Helena's somewhat battered one, Evan's duffle bag, reached into her purse for money.

"Hold it." Evan fumbled at his hip pocket. "We'll split three ways. Okay?"

"Oh, my, yes." Helena dug into a shoulder bag almost as large as she was.

"No, no, really, it's all right." The driver looked impatient and Cheryl handed him a bill. "Is that enough?"

"Fifteen dollars." He looked at her twenty.

"Haven't you any change?"

"Here," said Evan again. He had a five-dollar bill in his hand. The driver had a five-dollar bill, too. Helena made another move toward the shoulder bag.

"Never mind." Cheryl turned her back on the driver. "Keep it."

"Thank you, miss." The driver turned smartly and was out the door. The screen slammed behind him.

"Lindsay, darling." Helena had to lean back to look up into her friend's face. "You're looking wonderful except that you don't seem particularly happy to see me. Didn't Deirdre tell you I was coming?"

Lindsay Ball fluttered her hands. "Of course, I'm delighted to see you, Helena. It's just that I'm afraid I forgot to tell Florida and then there's two extra, as well . . ."

"Florida?"

"Florida, yes. She's the cook and Deirdre said we must all be responsible for something around the house—it's her theory, you see, she thinks we should be bored otherwise and so she put me in charge of menu planning because, she said, I'm so abysmal at it. And I protested, I really did, I told her I was quite good at flower arranging, couldn't I do that? But she said, no, I wouldn't learn anything new if I arranged flowers so even though the meals are sometimes quite strange, Deirdre says I shall improve and when I do, we'll have a celebration."

"Where is my—where is Deirdre?" Cheryl asked abruptly. Lindsay Ball sounded on the verge of being senile.

Lindsay looked vague, then brightened. "Didn't I tell you? She's having a massage. In the physical culture room." She lifted one arm like a grotesque ballet dancer, pointed down the hall. "It's the last door on the left, you can't miss it. I'll go and see if Florida has finished meditating. If she has, I'll tell her three more for dinner." And she floated away from them, murmuring to herself, "Three more for dinner. Three more for dinner."

"Perhaps it would be better if I waited here," Evan suggested. Helena had already started down the hall.

"Do as you like." Cheryl was regretting the fact that she'd let the driver get away with the car. If Lindsay Ball were a proper sample of the occupants of Belfry House, she wasn't at all sure she wanted to spend even one night under its roof. She followed Helena along the corridor, glancing into doorways as she passed. On the right, a large ornate room, living room it seemed, with a fantastic gold-framed mirror that covered almost an entire wall; on the left, a room that appeared to be a well-stocked library, its walls were covered with bookcases filled with books.

Beyond, on the right again, a dining room set up with separate tables, more like a hotel than a house; across the hall, could it be a theatre? No doubt, rows of chairs and a movie screen, it must be. Deirdre probably bored her captive audience with old Dunn films, the woman must have a tremendous ego.

And finally, yes, Helena had opened a door at the end of the hall, disappeared inside. Cheryl went after her, found herself in a high-ceilinged, square room. Gym mats covered the floor, ropes and rings hung from the ceiling and there was a table over by the windows, like an operating table in a hospital, and on it was a body covered with a sheet and standing over the table was a giant of a man, bare-chested in gym shorts, doing something to the body under the sheet on the table.

All Cheryl could see of the body was the head, and hanging down from the head was a single thick braid of hair. White hair. A long, lustrous braid of pure white hair. The color was so incongruous, it was almost obscene.

"Deirdre!" piped Helena in that squeaky voice. "Darling, I'm here!"

The unmistakable voice of Deirdre Dunn responded, even though the white head didn't turn. "Helena, it couldn't be anyone but you. Welcome."

"And I." Cheryl hadn't meant to speak so loudly.

Slowly, languorously, the body under the sheet turned, the head came around and Deirdre Dunn's nearly black eyes looked at Cheryl, recognized her, Cheryl could tell that, but the voice only said, "Oh?"

"Cheryl. Cheryl Harris." She stressed the word Harris bitterly.

"So it is. All right, Tony. That's enough." Swathing the sheet around her, Deirdre sat up. The famous Dunn eyebrows, like right and left acute accents done with a charcoal brush, moved up at each corner. Why should her hair be white and her eyebrows black? "This is a surprise."

"We met on the plane," Helena prattled. "Wasn't that a coincidence? And the young bat man, where is he?" She looked toward the door. "He came with us, too."

The brows moved even higher. "The young bat man?"

"He waited in the hall," Cheryl told her. "His name is Evan Garson."

Something moved behind the dark eyes, some sort of emotion showing itself for an instant, was banished to the depths.

"I had better get dressed then," said Deirdre matter-of-factly. She got off the table, the man Tony giving her a hand. She wore the sheet now like a toga, one end tossed over a shoulder. "Tony, take them to the living room and round up the lost bat man. I'll be there directly."

The big man, Cheryl guessed he was perhaps six feet seven or eight, basketball player height but heavier and considerably older than those giants, smiled and said, "Right this way, ladies." His voice was, surprisingly, tenor.

Helena trotted along beside him. The effect, the tiny and the very tall, was ludicrous. "How've you been, Tony?" she asked him, looking up, way up to see his face.

"All right, I guess. Getting older. Some of the parts don't work so well any more."

"Aren't we all? What I wouldn't give to start over again, pick it up when I was young, do it right the second time around."

Tony shook his big head. "Not me. No, ma'am. Probably just make the same mistakes. I'm not too bright, you know. Found that out as I went along. My mother said it, 'Tony, when brains were passed out you were behind the door.' Here we are, right in here. Is that your bat man down the hall? Come on down here, young fella. What can I get you folks while you're waiting? Hot or cold drink? Hard or soft? We've got 'em all."

"Nothing, thank you," Cheryl said coolly. Where had Deirdre picked this one up, she wondered. Mother—Alice—had had a friend who couldn't resist picking up stray cats. Deirdre's penchant seemed to be for human outcasts.

"Evan Garson"—Helena was doing the introductions—"this is Tony Nero. You've seen him on TV a million times but you may not know it."

Evan blinked up at Tony from behind the still-crooked glasses. "How are you?" he said, extending his hand.

Tony Nero smiled. His teeth were white, his skin dark,

Cheryl thought it a rogue's grin. "I was the talking robot. In all those commercials. The—one—that—talked—like—this. Only distorted and amplified. Remember?"

"Sure." Evan nodded foolishly. Cheryl had imagined the robot might be real. Well, it was possible. Television, where nothing was real. She sat down on a white and gold sofa under a Tiffany lamp. It was an elegant room, actually, even if untidy. The gold mirror needed polishing and the heavy lace curtains, draped at the sides with gold overdrapes, looked dusty. Someone had left a peculiar assortment over in one corner. A washtub, it looked to be, with a string attached to the middle of its upturned bottom, pulled taut by an upright stick. And a saw—and a bicycle pump?

"Oh," Helena spotted the wash tub. "Forrestor's paraphernalia. Where is he, anyway?"

"Probably having a nap," Tony told her. "Deirdre makes him lie down every afternoon. He's had a coronary, you know. She takes good care of us."

"Is that the lot?" asked Helena. "You and Forrestor and Lindsay?"

"No. Clive Keith is here and the Three Cuckoos. You know, Glen and Gene and George Hinkle. And"—he grinned, or was it leered—"Chrystal Clandestine."

"You're kidding!" Helena giggled.

Evan Garson looked interested. "Isn't she a burlesque dancer?"

"She sure was." Helena picked out a chair, sat in it, feet dangling. "Her real name is Gertrude something, but nobody's ever called her anything but Chrystal Clandestine for so long, everybody's forgotten. And the Hinkle brothers are the knock-down, drag 'em around comics, but I suppose you know that. Everybody's seen the Three Cuckoos at one time or another on the TV reruns of their three-reelers. And Clive, well, he's not so young any more but still he's the eternal sensitive young man, once billed as America's answer to Leslie

Howard. Quite a cast, we could put on a real extravaganza."

"Oh, we do occasionally. For our own amusement." Tony Nero folded himself, sat cross-legged on the floor with all the grace of a much younger man.

"But tonight is *Birth of a Nation,*" Deirdre spoke from the doorway. She was dressed in white, a sleeveless smocklike top over slacks. Her hair, almost as white as her costume, was braided coronet style atop her head, making her look taller. Cheryl wondered if she'd ever had her face lifted. "You must be the bat man," Deirdre said to Evan.

He attempted an inept bow. "I'm sorry to barge in on you, but you wouldn't answer my letters."

Deirdre's dark brows went up. "Letters?"

"Yes, I wrote you twice. I'm studying bats, I told you, doing research for a book and I'd heard about your bat colony . . ."

"Bat colony?" The brows changed shape, became a somehow attractive frown. "My bat colony? Here? Where did you ever get that idea?"

Evan looked somewhat abashed. "A friend of mine, was down here on vacation, he told me. Said Belfry House was locally famous for its bats."

Deirdre smiled. "Oh, that." She walked farther into the room, eyes amused. "That's one of those tales told to charm the tourists. And, to be frank, to keep them away. I thought of a ghost, but ghosts only attract the curious. Bats, now that's another thing entirely. I doubt that there's a woman in the world who isn't squeamish about bats."

Evan rubbed his nose in agitation, the glasses slipped askew. "You're telling me it isn't true? There aren't any bats in your tower?"

Deirdre put a sympathetic hand on his arm, a light touch. "It's extremely doubtful."

"Nobody's ever been up there as far as I know," Tony put in.

"Thank heavens!" Helena's ejaculation was fervent.

Evan looked thoroughly bewildered. "But my friend was so certain . . . would you mind if I went up and investigated?"

"Oh, I'm afraid that's impossible." Deirdre's tone left no doubt. "The only way up is by means of an old ladder and it's much too rickety. I couldn't allow it. It truly isn't safe." She turned now to Cheryl, there was a mesmeric quality in those dark eyes. "I'm so pleased to see you, my dear. But I fear you bring bad news. Has something happened to Alice?"

"She died two weeks ago." Cheryl heard her flat tone, was pleased at its lack of emotion.

The expressive Dunn face showed infinite sorrow. "She was one of my dearest friends," she explained to the room at large. "It must have been sudden?"

"Yes, very sudden." The bitterness showed now, Cheryl knew, but she couldn't control it. "If she'd been ill, she never told me. And one morning, I found her—dead. A stroke, the doctor said."

"She was so young," Deirdre murmured.

"She left a letter"—Cheryl's voice rose—"and she asked me to come and see you. So forgive me for not waiting for an invitation." This last, spoken sarcastically.

Deirdre looked directly into her eyes. "You are most welcome." She turned quickly to Evan Garson. "And you, too, young man, even though I haven't any bats for you. You will, at least, spend the night."

He made a futile attempt to straighten the perpetually crooked glasses. "I wouldn't want to put you out."

Deirdre laughed. "You wouldn't be putting me out at all. Now, Tony, let's find rooms for our guests. Cheryl in the blue room, I think, and there's no one in the third floor back, is there? Helena, I'd planned to put you next to Lindsay. If you'll just go with Tony, he'll handle your luggage. And when you're settled, Cheryl, would you come and see me? Tony will show you where. Otherwise, teatime is at four right here.

You'll meet everybody then. And"—she shared a dazzling smile with everyone—"be officially welcomed to Belfry House."

Cheryl rapped firmly on the white double doors and Deirdre's voice responded immediately. "Come in."

The room was a large corner one with four long windows on each of its two corner sides. The sun streamed through them onto a thick emerald green carpet, onto a huge round bed dressed in an ornate blue and green spread, made the white walls brilliant. There were many pictures on these walls, photographs of people. Famous people. Cheryl recognized many at a single glance.

Deirdre Dunn stood at one of the windows, face turned to see out. As Cheryl came in, Deirdre glanced over her shoulder at her and Cheryl saw another woman. Older. Sadder. The backstage Deirdre? How could one tell with a consumate actress?

"My dear granddaughter." Deirdre turned fully, put out her arms. "My dear."

Cheryl stayed where she was, in the middle of the lush green carpet. "I suppose you know that I hate you."

The arms dropped slowly, one corner of the mouth moved down, then up. "I can understand why you think you do," she said softly. "But believe me, I only tried to do what was best."

"Did you really?" Cheryl had to take deep breaths to keep from crying. "I don't care what your excuses are. One fact is obvious, you couldn't be bothered with me. So you farmed me out. That's all I came for, you see. To tell you that I hate you and always shall. You can shelter all the riffraff in the world, it seems, but not your granddaughter!" She clenched her hands at her sides. Tears mustn't come, she mustn't let them.

Deirdre turned back to the window. "Don't give me too

much credit for that," she said evenly. "I was lonely when I finally slowed down, retired. When I stopped running around the treadmill, I found I had nothing to do. So my charitable instincts are as much for myself as for anyone else."

"You could have sent for me." Cheryl couldn't keep herself from saying it, blurting the words out.

The white head moved from side to side. "No. It was too late. You were a teen-ager, you'd made your life with Alice. It would have been horribly unfair to both of you. I thought of it, often, believe me."

"I don't believe you."

The head tipped forward. "I suppose you think I've earned this." The head lifted, a brave gesture. Damn her and her practiced poses. "If you could only see—I was never in one place for longer than six months at a time. A child needs permanence, must go to school, make and keep friends . . ."

"A child needs family!"

"Yes. That's why Alice and I agreed that she would be your family. I assume she told you."

"She told me. In a letter."

Deirdre left that window, went to another. "I never expected it to come to this. I thought I'd paid my debt when I gave up all rights to you. Alice was younger, I considered that when I asked her, I thought you'd be an adult with children of your own when you found out, that you'd understand then because only when you've had children can you understand . . ."

Cheryl let the venom out. "I'm so sorry that your plans didn't work. It really is too bad to have a bitter granddaughter on your hands, isn't it? She could poison your pretty play, couldn't she? And you've written yourself such a good part, grande dame, lady of the manor, dispenser of largess. Deirdre Dunn, how noble, how fine! That's all I heard on the airplane down here. Well, I could have told them and maybe I will! I was going to tell you what I thought and then leave. But

I've changed my mind." Her face was flushed, she could feel it burn. "I'm going to stay around for a while and stick pins in your bubbles, that's what I'm going to do. My dear grandmother, this chicken's come home to roost!"

And she burst out through the tall double doors, ran down the hall to the room assigned to her, locked the door behind her, threw herself on the bed and burst into sobs.

Completely exhausted, she slept and when she awoke, the sun was on the horizon.

She was hungry. Other than that, she felt rested, oddly sure. She wasn't Deirdre Dunn's granddaughter for nothing. She was young and strong and driven by hatred. She'd make that hypercritical old woman rue the day she'd abandoned her. She stared at her face in the bathroom mirror and promised herself, she would, she would!

But she'd be clever about it. Catch more flies with sugar. Yes, she'd be very clever. She changed her rumpled dress, put on a bright flowered frock that had been the last dress she and Mother—damn it! Alice—had shopped for. "It makes you look like a spring sprite," Alice had told her. Her reflection satisfied her. Hair shining, smooth; cheeks pink, eyes bright. Ready to go downstairs and be charming. To all those—weird old people. Make friends. One by one. Anyone would feel sympathy for a young, pretty girl—Alice had said she was

35

pretty—and then, when they knew her better, knew how sweet and nice she could be, be won over, take sides if sides were to be taken.

Deirdre had been lonely, had she? She'd find out what lonely was!

Coming downstairs, Cheryl could hear voices but couldn't, at first, discover where the sounds came from. She walked past the gold and white room, empty; the dining room, glimpsed through its windows figures moving outside and guessed that there must be a patio of some sort beyond. French doors off the dining room led to it, it was really a large porch with an old-fashioned wooden railing, and Cheryl went out to it. Her grandmother was encircled, always stage center! She sat in a fan-backed wicker chair like a queen. Her long dress was of lavender silk jersey, she was animated, smiling. The smile wavered a fraction when she saw Cheryl and that waver pleased Cheryl.

"My dear, I don't believe you've met Forrestor McMann." Deirdre began the introductions with a red-cheeked, plump little old man who bobbed and beamed almost as though, thought Cheryl, he were simple-minded.

"And this is Chrystal Clandestine." Chrystal had red hair, as unbelievable as her name, hanging down her back in youthful ringlets. She also had a figure of amazing proportions.

"George," Deirdre went on, "where's Glen? There are three of them, Cheryl, this is George and this is Gene. Two of the Hinkle brothers better known as the Three Cuckoos."

Short wiry men with similar faces, only one was bald and the other had wild frizzy hair worn long, fanning out in all directions. "Hello." Cheryl smiled her best smile.

"And Lindsay . . ."

"We've met," said Cheryl. Another smile for Lindsay who had changed into yellow lace, yards of it, accented with pearls.

36

"And Clive Keith." A tall, regal-looking man with salt and pepper hair mounting in perfect waves, weary-looking eyes and a ravaged face. He must have been close to beautiful when he was young, Cheryl thought. But now, dissipated. Yes, definitely dissipated.

"I remember your movies," Cheryl lied.

"I think you know everyone else."

"Yes." More smiles for Helena, Evan, and Tony Nero. Evan was seated between Chrystal and Deirdre. She joined them, pulling a chair in between Evan and the Clandestine woman.

"Would you like a cocktail? Some wine?" asked Clive Keith. He stood by a portable bar, apparently his share-the-work role was that of bartender.

She looked deliberately demure. "Perhaps a glass of sherry?" She looked at Evan. "What are you drinking?"

He blinked. The epitome of the absent-minded professor. "Scotch, I think. To tell you the truth, I'm a non-drinker. Not against it, just never did it much. So you can't prove it by me." He grinned foolishly. Silly young man, she thought, would probably get smashed and make some sort of ass of himself. He seemed the type.

"After dinner, we're going to see *Birth of a Nation*," Helena bubbled. "Isn't that a treat?"

"Oh, yes." Cheryl tried to look properly impressed.

"You may think bats are dreadful"—Evan was talking across her to Chrystal—"but they're not, they're not at all. They eat enormous amounts of insects—mosquitoes, termites, moths, whatever. If only they could be persuaded to live on farms, in orchards, they'd be a boon to farmers and the answer for ecologists."

"Is that so?" Chrystal fluttered eyelashes that made Cheryl think of spiders. The redhead promptly began a conversation with one of the Hinkle brothers, the third one who'd come from somewhere. He had a peculiar haircut that looked as though it had been done with a bowl.

Evan, not a bit discouraged, focused his attention on Forrestor McMann. "The unique thing about Belfry House, or so I was led to believe, is that bats almost never gather in a colony in an inhabited house and in temperate climates. Older buildings suit them best, and when I saw this house I thought it looked uniquely ideal. The usual bat nuisances, odor and noise, would not be in evidence since the tower is separated from the living quarters."

Deirdre, overhearing, looked politely interested. "But they carry rabies," she said. "And who would encourage a rabies-carrying mammal to make its home in his home?"

Evan wagged a long, thin finger. "Now, that's not accurate, Miss Dunn. Misinformation. The world, it seems to me, is encouraged to discriminate against the bat. The number of rabies cases in this country attributed to bats is almost non-existent. More people die each year from bites from black flies or bee stings, did you know that? The only bat species known to be rabies-carriers is the vampire, principally in Mexico and Trinidad. And their victims are cattle, not men."

"Ah." Deirdre smiled mysteriously. "Shades of Count Dracula. Tell us terrible tales of the dreaded vampire."

"Desmodus rotundus." He now had the group's attention, his face flushed with enthusiasm. "Found in Mexico, Central, and South America. The common vampire has unusual teeth, two upper incisors, four small lower incisors, two upper and lower canines and ten cheek teeth. The incisors are used for biting the victim, the canines for defense. The vampire's diet is restricted to blood. He extends his tongue and curls its edges to form a tube."

"Ugh." Helena wrinkled her small nose.

"Maligned." Evan nodded his head wisely. "For one thing, no vampire bats have ever existed in Europe. So the Dracula legends are patently false. Vampire bats are small, weigh about an ounce, and they're timid. They rarely bite man because they're afraid of him. He's alert, you see, and what they do is walk up to their victim very quietly, yes, vampires can walk and jump, too, and they lick their victim before biting. It's not certain whether they do this to apply an anticoagulant or if they're testing the responses of the bitee, anyway if the response is sudden, they take off."

Lindsay bared her teeth, incisors and canines. "I find this conversation repulsive."

"In that case," Deirdre smiled at Evan—"we'll change the subject. Another time, another place, yes?"

"My pleasure. And if any of you are interested in studying the matter, there's a recent book called *The World of Bats* that should prove interesting. Dr. Alvin Novick does the text and there are splendid photographs by Nina Leen. I recommend it highly to laymen."

"Thank you, Mr. Garson." Deirdre rose, her retinue followed suit. "And now, shall we dine?"

Lindsay placed her hand on her stomach. "I don't know whether I can . . ."

Deirdre put a comforting arm around her shoulders. "Of course you can, my dear. What's on the menu this evening?"

"Oh"—Lindsay looked hopefully at Deirdre—"frogs legs. I thought it would be a nice change." And then she looked puzzled when everybody laughed.

Something seemed to be wrong with the projector and so they couldn't watch *Birth of a Nation* after dinner. They retired, instead, to the living room for liqueurs and coffee. They were served, as they had been at dinner, by a heavy-set silent woman Deirdre called Betsy. Cheryl hadn't seen any other servants, assumed there must be others in this big house, there was the cook for one, what was her name? Something improbable that went along with all the other improbabilities—oh, yes, Florida. Well, Florida was quite capable it seemed, dinner had been delicious. Cheryl sat back and sipped at a brandy without liking it much.

She watched them cluster around Deirdre, resented them and knew she was jealous. Only Evan was paying Cheryl any attention, he edged his chair closer to her now, eyes moist behind the glasses, perhaps he'd been drinking too much. Cheryl stood up, said quickly to anyone who would listen, "I haven't been to the beach yet. I think I'll go look at the ocean."

"I'll come with you," declared Evan.

"Cheryl, dear, where are you going?" Her grandmother must have eyes in the back of her head. Cheryl repeated her lame excuse to get away.

Deirdre looked concerned. "Do be careful. We are apt to have peculiar tides at peculiar times, it has something to do with the curvature of the earth or something. Anyway, we've had two instances of drowning in recent months. Take someone with you."

"Drownings? Who drowned?"

"That's just it, they were strangers and didn't know. So I always advise bathers to take someone with them."

"I'll escort Cheryl," Evan said grandly.

"In that case"—Deirdre seemed satisfied—"you'd better take your shoes off. There's an acre of dunes between the house and the sea."

"Great. Let's go wading." Evan Garson was already reaching down to his feet. Cheryl slipped off her sandals, placed them neatly under her chair. No one paid any attention to their going now, the others were involved in a trivia game, something about old movies, hardly fair, Deidre must know all the answers.

The evening air was soft and the horizon was a marvelous painting done in golds and purples. Strands of dune grass did sinuous dances in the small breeze. The sand felt cool to her feet, she moved across it easily. She could hear Evan breathing hard behind her. Out-of-shape scientist.

"Look!" he said suddenly. "Up there!"

She turned her head to see. A shadow, a bird, moved against the fiery lavender sky. "What is it?"

"A bat. A pipistrellus, I believe. I was right! There are bats at Belfry House." He stood enraptured, watching. Cheryl shuddered involuntarily. The shadowy winged form soared effortlessly out of sight.

Evan turned his back on Cheryl, stared at the house behind them. Bright lights shone from the first floor, there were softer lights in various rooms on the upper floors, but the tower was dark. The sky was dark now, too, suddenly. The grayness of the house blended into it, made the window lights look brighter.

Evan Garson began to run toward the house, he slipped in the soft sand, righted himself.

"Where are you going?" Cheryl called after him.

"To tell her . . . wait," his voice trailed after him.

Idiot, thought Cheryl and shrugged, went on her way to the sea. It was, by the time she reached it, a black and silver sea. Its surface, agitated by the breeze which had freshened, broke up into curls, white curling fingers that flung themselves on the beach to die there. The moon was cold and round. Cheryl hitched up her skirt and walked into the sea, walked only a little way until the water reached mid-calf and sometimes splashed her, wetting her dress hem. She didn't care.

Someone called her name and broke the spell. She looked back to the beach, Evan was there, a scarecrow in the night.

She didn't answer and he came toward her, rolling up his pants legs as he came. When he was at the tidemark where she could hear, he said, "I don't understand her."

And Cheryl, unmoving, asked, "Deirdre Dunn?"

"Oh, she says there could have been a bat. One, maybe.

But she says the other ones, the ones I saw leaving the tower, she says that couldn't be. She wouldn't even come look, but I suppose it would have been too late, anyway. They make a general exodus." Now in the water, a wave spanked him, he moved unvoluntarily backward. "But you saw them."

She hadn't seen anything except the shape that could have been a bird. "Of course."

"I wonder why . . ."

"She doesn't want people to know she has bats in her belfry." She laughed at the moon.

"I suppose so. Still, she seems to be such a reasonable, practical lady. And intelligent, too. You'd think she could take me aside if she doesn't want to disturb the others, I wouldn't be obvious. I'd just go up into the tower when no one was around . . . perhaps she doesn't understand that." He straightened his glasses, using one hand that had been clutching a trouser leg, as a result the leg slipped down, was sopped by the sea. "That's the mistake I made," he said, groping for the trouser leg, "in my enthusiasm I went on about them in front of the others. Tomorrow I shall speak to her alone, explain that I won't upset anyone, I'll be as quiet as a vampire when it sneaks up on its prey."

Cheryl came out of the water. Back against the dunes were some beach chairs, she set one straight, sat in it, stared up at the fascinating moon.

"Perhaps you don't know what a pipistrellus is." Evan, indomitable, dragged another beach chair up, awkwardly tried to set it straight.

"What did you say? Oh—no, I don't know what a pipistrellus is, another of your bats, I presume."

"It's a member of the Vespertilionidae, the most common of the Chiroptera, pardon, bats. They, along with the Myotis and Epetesicus, range worldwide. The Lasiurus, red and hoary bats, are liable to be in this part of the world, too. They live in the U.S. and Canada in the summer and migrate

42

south in the winter. The Vespertilionidae have the facility to drop their body temperatures to that of the environment, which is . . ."

"Evan, please. I don't want a lecture on bats. Can't you talk about anything else? What do you think of these people, for instance? Aren't they strange?"

"Strange?" The moonlight made his lenses silver. "I suppose they might be to a non-theatrical person. But to me, it's like a convention of scientists. You should see some of them when they get together, all riding special hobbyhorses." He laughed. "Dr. Birker, for instance, when he comes off one of his trips, he's usually been in the field for months, he looks like the hairy ape personified . . ."

"I don't understand what you want here. You say there are bats in the tower. So what if there are? Why come all the way from wherever you came from, barge in uninvited, just to look at some common ordinary bats? You said they were common, can't you go study them someplace else?"

He leaned forward, the moonlight left his eyes and she could see the inner gleam in them. "I'll try and make you understand about the scientist. There's so much to be learned—over twelve hundred species and subspecies have been observed and there must be many more, we just don't know. Their sonar systems, their temperature regulations, their longevity, their mobility . . . and then there's the relatively sparse bat population in the temperate zones. I could go on and on—so much to be discovered. And here, or so I am told by a fellow physiologist who summered here, is a rare situation, an inhabited dwelling housing a bat colony. Why? And are these bats members of the Vespertilionidae family? Is there a nursery colony up in that tower?"

He took a breath. "A scientist's curiosity is close to an emotion, nearly insatiable." He looked embarrassed, laughed. "I do get carried away."

"But Dierdre says . . ."

He waved his hands in negation. "I don't believe her."

"But why would she lie?"

"I told you. Man has an inherent aversion to bats. Have you ever looked at one up close? They are, at least to me, quite attractive. Better looking than some dogs and cats I've seen. An animal with wings, absolutely unique."

Cheryl thought his passion ridiculous and because she couldn't tell him that, she said nothing, just nodded and looked to the sea.

He surprised her by asking, "And why are you here?"

"I?"

"You are not, obviously, a child of the theatre. And I gather you came uninvited as well, although you seem to be more welcome than I."

Coolly, "My mother was Deirdre's close friend. She died recently. I came to tell Deirdre."

"I see. I'm very sorry about your mother."

"Thank you."

"How long will you be staying?"

"I'm not sure."

"If you have any influence, I'd appreciate any efforts on my behalf."

"You're determined to go up into that tower?" She looked back toward the house, could barely make out the dark shape of the belfry above the sand dunes, against the dark sky.

"Oh, yes. It seems such a simple request. I can't imagine why she refuses."

"She says it isn't safe."

"Yes, I know. But I'd be careful—and I'd free her from any responsibility."

Unexpected sounds came then, abruptly, there was quiet and then there was a thumping rhythm, musical strains came over the dunes, voices. Startled, Cheryl got up from her chair, "What in the world . . . ?"

44

"It sounds as though they're putting on an entertainment. Let's go see. I'm like a big kid when I go to the theatre."

Cheryl came after him slowly, moved faster when she saw that he waited impatiently for her. If her grandmother hadn't abandoned her, she'd have known this peculiar world, have been at ease, maybe even shared it.

She'd been cheated. Truly cheated. And that she would never forgive.

Euderma maculata, *the spotted bat has tremendous ears which can be unfurled. He is marked with three white spots on his dark back, probably for camouflage.*

Evan . . .

He hoped he'd convinced her. She behaved as though she hadn't a brain in her pretty head, feisty little babe, sour disposition, she'd be a beauty if she had a personality and if she ever smiled.

But most of all, he hoped he'd convinced Deirdre Dunn. He was sound on the bat bit, why shouldn't he be? His father, Dr. Elias Garson, was the expert, some of his speeches verged on remembered quotes from his father. And then he'd worked with the experts himself at Harvard to earn his way through law school. But the bumbling, eager young scientist act—was he overlaying it? He hoped not. He thought not. The cast of characters at Belfry House seemed gullible enough.

Deirdre Dunn's reaction was the one that puzzled him.

Puzzle A: Why no reply to the carefully coached letters, not even a polite no-no, a thousand times no?

Puzzle B: Why, when Evan Garson, "scientist," did show up was he invited to stay, at least overnight?

And, Puzzles C and D (should really be rated at the top of the list): Did one Alvaro Rojas, gardener by profession, and one Cecilia Jenks, housemaid, die by accidental drowning off Belfry House within eighteen months of each other?

Possible answers: A—somewhat scatter-brained actress takes cavalier attitude toward unsolicited correspondence.

B—Hostess with the mostest acts sincere, can't turn away strays.

C and D—Yes, yes. Alvaro Rojas, immigrant from Portugal, foolhardy about sea, didn't know tides. Cecilia Jenks, described as less than bright, unathletic. (Which brought up another question: If unathletic, what was she doing out at Belfry House point anyway? There were safer, better beaches all over the place.)

It had been Jim Harding's idea.

"Jim," he'd protested, "this whole thing seems unnecessarily elaborate to me. Chief Griffin down in Truro smells something funny, I know, but aren't we setting up a sticky game plan? Me, I'm all for the direct approach. Madame, do you or someone in your household have a fondness for killing off the help? I thought maids and gardeners were pretty hard to get these days."

Jim Harding, an assistant to the State Attorney General of Massachusetts, generally noted for a lack of a sense of humor, found Evan's speech non-funny. In fact, he frowned. "You gave me the idea for this thing yourself."

"I know, I know. You asked me if I had any ideas as to how to get into Deirdre Dunn's house and I went off on one of my tangents and plotted a way for you. But I didn't think you or Ben or anyone else with any sense would take it seriously." And he couldn't resist adding, "Even if you bought it, I felt safe with Ben. Our Attorney General is a vastly practical man."

Jim's frown had deepened. "When you get polite inquiries from the State House, you jump, froggy. There's a Portuguese Ambassador in Washington who knows a senator who knows a governor . . ."

"I get the picture, believe me. The ambassador has friends in Portugal, too, and someone wasn't unhappy when Alvaro's body turned up as food for fishes. Nobody fusses so much about the Jenks girl, who was she anyway, only the school custodian's daughter . . ."

"Evan"—Jim Harding had looked pained—"there are times when it's all I can do to take you."

And he'd grinned; he might not amuse Jim but Jim sure as hell amused him. "All right, uncle, uncle. I'll purloin some of the old man's official stationery and we'll send off a letter to Deirdre Dunn. Dear Miss Dunn, may I come see your bats?" He turned serious. "Chief Griffin is sure about that, is he? They don't normally hang out in inhabited buildings. Either the people get rid of the bats or the bats get rid of the people."

"You say nobody cares about the Jenks girl, well, Chief Griffin does, she was the daughter of his cousin. And she told her father that she was scared of the bats at Belfry House. Besides, it's common talk in the town. If she lived in close to people, somebody might take it to the Board of Health, but she's got that old house sitting way out there in the dunes, so who cares, that's the attitude of the townspeople. If some crazy actress wants to raise bats on her place, that's her business. Besides, they don't want to scare her off. They're proud of the fact that the great Deirdre Dunn has settled down in their little town."

Which brought up Puzzle E: Could the famed Miss Dunn be encouraging a bat colony in her house? If so, why?

She'd given him a reason. To keep the curious away. Only, she'd denied the actual existence of the bats, described the story as a deliberate rumor, or intimated same.

Which brought him to Puzzle F: Were there actually bats in Belfry Tower? The flying object he'd pointed out to Cheryl Harris might or might not have been. His eyesight wasn't that good at that distance, he'd simply used the opportunity to push the contention.

Leading to Puzzle G: Why did he feel so strongly that the bat bit had anything at all to do with a pair of accidental drownings? That was the nut that bothered him. His job called for a lot of law, a minor in psychiatry, a curiosity bump the size of a mountain, and a full measure of hunch material. Only this was—a sign of softening of the brain or hardening of the arteries?

Well, he'd find out about the bats if nothing else. With permission, or without. At night? When all were abed? We-ll. The furry little mammals would be off flying and feeding. But there would be evidence. Guano. The unmistakable bat odor. This night? Play it by ear. Wait and see what Deirdre's attitude toward the slightly mad young scientist would be in this eighth—or ninth?—hour since their meeting.

He ushered the suddenly silent Cheryl in through the French doors in rhythm to the whack-whack-whack made by the little old man, Forrestor what's-his-name playing a pair of spoons by thumping them against his knee.

The golden age club in action . . . "When you wore a tulip, a big yellow tulip, and I wore a big red rose . . ." One of the look-alike except for the hairdos Hinkles was doing, falsetto-voiced, an imitation of Tiny Tim.

Small Helena lifted her skirts and tap-danced on the marble hearth of the fireplace, the ghost of a *Follies* girl came to life as Lindsay began the exaggerated walk he'd seen only in films; they were rapt in concentration, they were entertaining themselves. It was somehow piteous and wonderful.

The rest, spectators, applauded when the performances ended. Cheryl clapped her hands politely. Dead fish. He was more enthusiastic, he was pretty sure Deirdre was watching, besides he had enjoyed it.

Deirdre, the mother figure with her old children. Odd that he thought that. There wasn't anything very motherly about her. She was, in his opinion, quite beautiful. Exciting. She would be, he supposed, until the day she died.

"May I play in your yard?" Evan asked. "I only know one song, had to learn it for a college show, but it might make you laugh." They were so charming, so unself-conscious doing "their thing." For the first time he saw them as larger than life, figures from the screen in full three dimension. He felt a sudden and foolish affection for them all. The old dears. Acting out yesterday.

Helena clapped her hands in pleasure and Deirdre said, "Oh, yes, sing it, please."

Evan cleared his throat. "Remember, I'm a rank amateur. Here goes—a cappella and, no doubt, flat—it's a sentimental ballad, as you will see, by Tom Lehrer.

"About a maid I'll sing a song,
    sing rickety-tickety-tin,
    about a maid I'll sing a song
    who didn't have her family long,
    not only did she do them wrong,
    she did everyone of them in, them in,
    she did everyone of them in."

He looked quickly at their faces, he didn't seem to be doing too badly, they all looked amused and interested.

"One morning in a fit of pique,
    sing rickety-tickety-tin,
    one morning in a fit of pique
    she drowned her father in the creek,

53

the water tasted bad for a week,
and we had to make do with gin, with gin,
we had to make do with gin.

"Her mother she could never stand,
sing rickety-tickety-tin,
her mother she could never stand
and so a cyanide soup she planned.
Her mother died with the spoon in her hand
and her face in a hideous grin, a grin,
her face in a hideous grin."

Helena, bless her gentle heart, was put off by that part, he
could see. She wore a rather hideous grin herself at that moment. He smiled reassuringly at her.

"She set her sister's hair on fire,
sing rickety-tickety-tin,
she set her sister's hair on fire
and as the smoke and flame rose high'r,
danced around the funeral pyre,
playing a violin—olin,
playing a violin.

"She weighted her brother down with stones,
sing rickety-tickety-tin,
she weighted her brother down with stones
and sent him off to Davy Jones.
All they ever found were some bones,
and occasional pieces of skin, of skin
and occasional pieces of skin."

Oh, oh, that verse was near the mark, wasn't it? Perhaps
that's the reason he'd volunteered to sing it. He watched their
expressions, got no message from any of them.

"One day when she had nothing to do,
    sing rickety-tickety-tin,
    one day when she had nothing to do,
    she cut her baby brother in two,
    and served him up as Irish stew
    and invited the neighbors in, -bors in,
    invited the neighbors in."

Song over, he made an exaggerated bow and received applause. Helena made a face at him. "That's a terrible song."

"That's all right," he countered, "I'm a terrible singer." They laughed at that.

"I must go to bed," said Deirdre, rising. "Now that the *pièce de résistance* is over."

He looked at his watch. Only 9:45. Perhaps that was the way she retained that peculiar youthful quality. Early to bed and early to rise? No one seemed surprised at her announcement, it was obviously routine.

"Good night," he said, "and thank you."

She looked at him with those bottomless dark eyes and he had a fleeting moment of guilt. Could she see into his head? Of course not, it was only that she had that way of looking at a person.

When she had gone, leaving the others, the feeling changed. Cheryl was looking after her hostess, staring at the doorway she'd gone through. Her expression puzzled him— almost as though there was an animosity . . . strange. What could the girl have against Deirdre Dunn? The others seemed to worship the woman, if not worship then something very akin. The mother image came back to him, but no, that wasn't it. Not child to mother, more like pupil to teacher? Subjects to queen? Not those either. There was a subtlety here that eluded him.

Tony Nero suggested, "Maybe I can fix the projector and we can watch a Deirdre picture."

"Shhh," cautioned Lindsay. "Don't let her hear you."

"What do you mean, don't let her hear you?" Cheryl frowned at Lindsay.

"It's verboten," Clive Keith explained. "She won't let us show them. She says it's like watching the dead."

"I'll give you a hand with the projector," Evan offered. "Sometimes I'm good with things mechanical."

"Oh, Tony can fix anything," Chrystal told him.

"I'm tired." Cheryl got out of her chair. "I'm going to bed, too."

"Pleasant dreams." Helena sounded almost happy to be rid of her. "Good night," the others murmured and then came in a body after Tony and Evan, seeking further amusement. They quipped among themselves as they fiddled with the projector. "There's a slippage somewhere," Tony reasoned, "we need a screwdriver . . ."

One of the Hinkles fetched the required tool. Clive Keith was telling a bawdy British story, their voices were louder now, they laughed louder. Evan suddenly imagined hand-made dolls in some old-fashioned toyshop, relaxing after the toymaker had gone to bed.

The film was an old one, Evan had never seen it but he'd heard of it. It was a horror movie about bats. For his benefit? Fine.

It wasn't the original *Dracula*, Deirdre hadn't appeared in that one; it was a sequel done a few years later and not so popular as the first, at least that's what Tony said.

Good, though, Evan thought, watching. Bela Lugosi was the Count, but then wasn't he always? And Deirdre, young, not beautiful as he had imagined she had been, too thin and uncertain, but so very vulnerable. She made him long to protect her. That had been her extraordinary talent, then, at least at this stage in her career.

Clive slipped out and brought brandies when Tony changed

reels. Evan, sipping and watching, was aware of how much he was enjoying himself.

And what did all this have to do with the accidental deaths of two very obscure people?

Nothing. Nothing at all. Somebody was way off base.

When the picture was finished, Chrystal turned on the lights and began to collect glasses. Lindsay yawned, covered it with a beringed hand. "We've got to pick up," Tony told her.

"I'm so weary." She drooped in her chair, a dramatic drooping.

"Let me help." Evan had never felt so awake in his life. He'd brought a flashlight, never a better time to make a trip to the tower when everyone was in bed, answer the question of bats or no bats, then get out and leave these people alone.

What did bats have to do with anything anyway? He couldn't give himself a sensible reason, it was just that Deirdre had been so adamant . . . Garson, old boy, he told himself, you're getting soft. Give the thing up and go home. Tell Jim Harding the whole bit is wacked up.

"If you'll empty the ashtrays . . ." Chrystal smelled of some real zingy perfume. He'd seen her in Boston in action once, when he was in school. He and a couple of his friends had skipped classes, gone to see the burly-cue, it was a dying art if art was the word for it.

The chorus line had been a great disappointment; the comics weren't very funny; but Chrystal had come up to expectations. He wondered if he should tell her, decided against it. He emptied ashtrays.

"I'll vacuum tomorrow," said Chrystal.

"You'll what?"

"Vacuum. That's my job. Picking up, dusting, and vacuuming the public rooms." She gave him a make-something-of-it look.

He did. "Doesn't Betsy—isn't she the one who served dinner?—or somebody else do that?"

"She can't do this whole house. Besides, Deirdre says it's good for us to be busy." Chrystal lowered her incredible eyelashes, murmured, "But personally I'd like to keep busy doing something else." She didn't spell out the something else, but Evan got a rough idea.

"Lights out?" asked Tony from the doorway, hand on switch.

"We're coming," Chrystal told him. The others had gone.

"You mean Betsy is the only one?"

"Betsy and Florida, the cook. They've been with Deirdre for years and years."

"But a big house like this—how come?"

"It's hard to get help these days, you know. Everybody's going to college." She pronounced it something like collitch.

Evan wondered if the dearth of help had anything to do with money. It must cost a pretty penny to run this place, feed these people . . . "How long have you been here?"

She thought. "Nearly a year. God, is it that long?"

"Hey, if you two are going to talk all night, turn out the lights, will you?" Tony was still in the doorway.

"Sure." Chrystal waggled a reassuring finger at him and he left. Evan got the idea that he left reluctantly.

"Do you remember a maid named Cecilia?"

"Cecilia?" She frowned. "Gee, I don't know—we had two or three at one time, but they didn't stick it. What did she look like?"

He'd seen pictures, read the description. "About five feet-two or -three, thin, light brown hair."

"Kinda dumb-looking?"

"Could be."

"Yeah. She was only here a couple of days. Seemed scared to death of her own shadow, I remember now. Deirdre had to fire that one. She broke a bunch of Deirdre's good china."

"I see." He didn't see. The girl's father, nor the chief, had said nothing about Cecilia losing her job. Could be she didn't tell him, afraid to, maybe. Evan hadn't talked to the man personally, had read Chief Griffin's report.

"How'd you know Cecilia, anyway?" Chrystal threw back a lock of red hair with a toss of her head.

"Oh. Well, you remember I said I had a friend who summered in Truro, the one who told me about the bats? Well, he went around with her and that's how he found out about the bats. Cecilia told him."

"You're kidding." She looked ceilingward. "You mean there really are bats in this place?"

"That's what she said."

"Well, I sure wouldn't take her word for it. She looked to me like she'd been out of school when they passed out sense. You ready for beddy-bye?" She was standing quite near, that perfume was something.

"If you are." No hurry, had to allow time for heads to hit pillows, sleep to come. He wondered if Chrystal remembered the gardener—no, that had been almost two years ago. Besides, don't push luck. It would be a bit sticky to explain how he'd heard of Rojas. And while Chrystal was on the dese and dose side, she was no dumbbell.

"Yeah, I guess I am. Kind of beat. When I was younger I could make the whole night, you know? But now . . ." She shrugged, walked to the doorway. "Don't forget the light. Deirdre's generous but she goes bananas when we waste stuff."

He obediently snapped the switch and followed her down the dimly lit hall. "What about those lamps?"

"There's a master switch at the foot of the stairs. Wait till I'm partway up, will you? I don't like it down here when it's dark."

He watched her climb. "Why's that?" His voice was deliberately casual.

She stopped, turned, looked past him to the corridor. "I

don't know. I never thought about why. I just don't like it. It's a big house, you know. Old. It's like . . ." She stretched her imagination as far as it would go. "There are things in it that maybe have been here a long time. Longer than us." She started up, she'd had enough of that. "I just don't like it when it's dark. Lots of people don't like the dark."

He saw Chrystal to her room, it was on the third floor as his was, but on the front side of the house.

"Good night," she said, smiling. There was a trace of the coquette left in the smile, in the pale light she looked almost young, sexy. "I thought that song of yours was a real gas." He wondered if she were trying to keep him there, talking. "Will you teach me the words tomorrow?"

He thought he'd better go. "Sure. Good night, Chrystal."

She hummed, "She did everyone of them in," went inside and closed the door. Softly.

Evan paused before his own door, the house seemed quiet. No, there was water running someplace, he could hear it in the pipes. And a slit of light crawled over a threshold, from whose room he wasn't sure. Small bulbs lit the hallway at intervals, Chrystal hadn't said anything about turning those off, apparently they were night lights that stayed on. He checked his watch again, too early yet. Another half hour or so. Let's not get sleepy now, he told himself.

He went into his room, stood by the window that faced oceanward. He couldn't see the water but he could hear it faintly. He pulled a chair to the window, sat in it. Staring into the night would keep him awake. He couldn't see much, the moon had been covered by clouds, in for the night it looked like. Rain tomorrow? Could be.

He nodded, just once he thought, but when he looked at his watch again, its luminous dial told him almost an hour had passed, it was a quarter past one. He stood, stretched, got his flashlight from the pocket of his duffle bag. He opened his door a crack, listened.

Silence. Comfortable silence.

He had sneakers on, no sound except on a couple of the stair treads. Each time that happened he hesitated, listened, had anyone heard?

No.

In the lower hall, he went to the door on the left, one he hadn't entered, that hadn't been opened at all in his presence. He'd figured it out, though, while he'd waited there that afternoon, he'd even turned its knob, cracked it, and saw another hall leading to the center portion of the house. He'd closed the door again quickly so as not to disturb the dust on the floor. No one had been in there, it seemed, not for some time.

Well, if he left footprints now, he'd just have to leave footprints. Besides, he intended to tell Deirdre. "I hope you don't mind, it was safe enough after all, and there are no bats, you were right." Or, "There are bats, my friend was right." Whichever way, if she didn't want anyone in there, she should lock the door. He wondered fleetingly why she didn't.

He played his light ahead. It was more than a hall, actually, more of a passageway, maybe twenty feet wide and apparently connecting the two wings and offering entrance to the tower. The only doors were the one behind him and one ahead. A ladder, literally a ladder, rose from the center wall up into the darkness.

Evan passed it by, tried the door at the end. This wing was for the servants, someone had indicated, so it would be largely unoccupied. Its door was locked. Good enough. He went back to the ladder and sent his light up.

Straight up. The light wasn't powerful enough to illuminate the top. No landings along the way that he could see. Strange sort of arrangement. He wondered why it was built that way. If the tower were ever used, it would require a staircase. Climbing this thing called for some athletic ability. Deirdre hadn't been putting him off arbitrarily. It did look tricky. He studied the rungs on the lower level. Old, dusty, even cobwebby but sturdy enough. He put the light on the floor, put both hands on the uprights of the ladder and shook it. Not too rickety. Must be affixed to the wall all the way up, had to be. He used the light again, yes, by wrought-iron brackets.

Well, here goes . . . he should have brought a flashlight with a handle, but with sour milk, no crying. Grasping the lamp and ladder sides, hard to keep the light straight as he went, holding it and one side together, easy now, no hurry . . . he started up.

One rung at a time, that's the way . . . one rung, two rungs, three rungs . . . it was hot in there, no air, he started to perspire. His hands were sweaty, for God's sake, don't drop the light. Hold it now, hang on, an arm over the rung, wipe the light on your shirt, hands, too, there, that's better.

Up. Don't look down. Don't look down. He looked down— pitch black. He must be about halfway. What the hell was he doing here anyway? Some nutsy idea he'd got in his head that connected a tower, bats, and two drowned people. Wild. Out of it. Definitely, positively stark-raving mad.

But—he was halfway up. It was just as far to the top as it was to the bottom.

He kept going. A little easier now. Second wind. And besides, it was cooler up here, there must be air coming from someplace. Hold it! He froze on the ladder. Was that a sound? What kind of a sound? From below or above? A murmur, like a human voice? A woman's voice? Of course not. If anything, a bat squeak. Maybe a nursing mother of a bat, disturbed by her sucking child . . .

He reached up again, must be near the top now, if he could flash the light up, but he might drop it, careful, another rung, reach up . . . a creak?

Was there a creaking in the ladder? Oh, my God, it's giving way, the rung is going, the one I'm standing on, the whole thing, hang on, hang on, grab, grab, the light, grab . . . anything, anything!

Grab, damn you, grab!

Pteropus . . . the largest of the
flying fox have wing spreads
of four to five feet and
may weigh two pounds or
more. Their bodies, excluding
the wings, are like those of
large pigeons. They feed on
fruit and flowers.

Chrystal . . .

Chrystal said her prayers when she got into bed. She had never missed a nightly prayer since she was a very little girl. She'd learned to do it silently so that no one would know. There had been people in her life who would have laughed at her, hooted, had they known. So she prayed silently, efficiently.

She prayed because she believed that no matter how bad she was, it was all right as long as she said she was sorry.

Prayers being the second part of her nightly routine (face cream, chin strap, hairpins, etc., being the first), she went on to the third—writing. She opened the jewel case she kept locked and took out the diary. Not many "jewels" left, plenty of room for the diary.

It was a five-year diary dated 1948 through 1952 but she didn't care that the dates were wrong. She didn't write the way one was supposed to write in a diary, today I did this . . . etc. She wrote memories as they came to her. She had the book half-filled by now. When she ran out of space, she'd have to do something about getting another diary. Would Deirdre give her the money for that?

She'd started the writing by accident. Doing the chores, cleaning one day in the basement storeroom, Deirdre had said to her, "Really, Chrystal, don't complain that there's nothing to do. Find something to do. There's plenty of work about, a little work never hurt anyone. Take your mind off—things." And, annoyed, no, more than annoyed, just plain mad, she'd gone off into the basement as far as she could get away from Deirdre who was so damned bossy just because she was paying the bills.

There were lots of rooms down in the basement, a room for the big, old furnace that looked like a fat man in a plaster cast and that ate coal in the winter, and a room for tools and a room for wine, yet, and this storeroom where all the trunks and suitcases were kept.

Well, she'd picked that one because it was the least cobwebby and she'd found the diary in an old suitcase she'd never seen before, one with straps on it, must contain some of Deirdre's junk. Some old dresses and a pair of ice skates, of all things, and some odds and ends and the diary.

There was some scribbling in the front of it. January 1, 1948, through January 10, all filled in, then a page here and there for the next few months. Chrystal could imagine how that had happened. A new diary, a New Year's resolution, I will write every day, and then lost interest. But it didn't read like Deirdre's diary, must have been someone else's . . . "He has asked me to marry him and Mother is thinking it over . . ." the he underlined on every page. *He* did this and *he* did that and Mother still hadn't given her permission until May of 1948, the last entry. "Mother said yes! She said I could marry *him*. I don't know why she took so long, she wouldn't give me a reason, but now I don't care! I am so happy! I am so happy!"

Well, Chrystal was glad *she* was happy, whoever *she* was,

so she left those pages in and wrote her thoughts after that. It was strange, how easy it was to write. She'd never been very good at spelling and she'd never been any good at all doing essays and all that stuff in school, but she got a real kick out of doing this. She was careful about her handwriting, too, make it look pretty, o's over the i's instead of dots, and little hearts for o's, nice in words like love.

This day she'd been thinking about Timmy. She'd decided to write him a letter. Of course, he'd never see it unless there was any truth to that stuff about looking down from heaven and seeing everything so clear. If he was in heaven. Well, why shouldn't he be? He wasn't that bad a guy. And, being Catholic, he'd gone to church a lot. If he'd confessed his sins like he was supposed to, why shouldn't he be in heaven?

"Dear Timmy," she wrote and sat nibbling the end of her ball-point pen. Then, might as well say it right off . . . "I never did get a chance to tell you how sorry I am about what happened. Maybe you know anyway, but I've got to tell you, I never meant to do it. It was an accident. That's all, an accident. Believe me, nobody shed more tears than I did at your funeral.

"You got to take part of the blame, too, you know. If you hadn't been playing around with that Dolores Vonn, it never would have happened. I mean, you know I got a temper, and you know I've got my pride, too. What ever did you see in her anyway? I didn't think she was so hot, she was too fat for one thing, those big boobs and all, that was just plain fat. And she was no good, you know that, or you should. You weren't the only one she was putting out to. She wasn't nothing like me, with me it was only one man at a time, but with her it was anybody!

"And, on top of that, you shouldn't have left your gun at my place. I know you trusted me and all that, you had good reason to trust me, but when I found out about you and that Dolores, there it was, the gun with bullets in it and everything and naturally it came to me that I could use it to scare you off her, just scare you, that's all I meant to do.

"So when you came in that morning, pussy-footing, I'd been waiting up for you all night, there I was sitting in the dark in that chair with your gun in my hand and I said, where have you been and you said, playing poker with the boys and I said, you damned liar and you said, what are you talking about and I said, I'm talking about that bitch Dolores Vonn, that's who I'm talking about and you said, smart-ass like, oh yeah, what about her?

"You shouldn't have said that, Timmy. You should have kept on lying because, to tell you the truth, I would have believed you if you had, I wanted to believe you. But you did say it, you said what about her and I got up from that chair, there were skyrockets in my head, I was so mad and the next thing I knew you were trying to grab the gun from me and pushing me around and the gun went off.

"Bang! I can still hear the sound of it. I couldn't see your face, it wasn't light yet, but I felt you move away from me and I heard you grunt and fall. I ran to put on the light and when I leaned over you you were dead as a doornail already, lying there with your eyes open, your beautiful baby blue eyes, looking so surprised.

"Well, I cried and cried. I cried my head off but it didn't do any good. I called Deirdre, she was my friend, thank God, and her apartment was upstairs and she knew all the big shots, was going around with some lawyer at the time, and I told her I'd shot you and she came right down.

"She looked at you and she said you sure were dead and I said I knew that, what should I do? So she said she'd call her lawyer friend and then the police so the lawyer would have a head start and we'd say it was self-defense because it was your gun.

"And I said, what do you mean, self-defense? And she said, he came in and tried to beat you up. And I said, well, he pushed me around some but he didn't beat me up, it was only an accident, couldn't we tell them that?

"But she said they wouldn't believe that because of who I was and because of who you were, Timmy, a gangster. That's what she called you. I told her you weren't a gangster, you just did a little bootlegging and she just stood there shaking her head.

"So I said, if he was supposed to beat me up—meaning you—shouldn't I look beat up? And she said, yes, I should. So you know what she did? She hauled off and hit me in the eye with her fist, my God, she hit me hard, you would have thought she was a man. She knocked me down with that blow and I started to bawl and she hit me again!

"Then, cool as ice, she called her lawyer friend and told him to come over 'cause her friend had killed a man in self-defense and then she called the cops. By the time the cops got there, we had the story all set and boy, anybody would have believed it with my silk robe all torn and my black eye and the crying and carrying on I did. So that's how I got off scot-free and for a while after that I was really raking in the dough because everybody wanted to see Chrystal Clandestine who shot her boy friend in self-defense."

Chrystal put her pen down and sighed, lit a cigarette. It had been so long ago, but she remembered as though it was yesterday. Gertrude Muscort and Deirdre Dunn, that was Deirdre's real name, spelled just like that, which was fine for the stage but not Gertrude Muscort, God no, they'd been a couple of kids then trying to make it big. Well, in some ways they both had made it big; Deirdre bigger than Gertrude— Chrystal. Deirdre had made it real big.

Class, that's what she'd had even then. No two ways about it. The way she'd stood there that night and socked Chrystal in the eye. Wow, she'd never forget that. Saved her life probably, now was saving it again. Because all that dough had just slipped through Chrystal's fingers somehow. And now, face it, when she was getting to be an old bag, Deirdre gave her a home.

She should get down on her knees and kiss Deirdre's feet, she knew she should. If only—damn it, why did she feel so trapped, like in a prison? "Better not hang around Truro, Chrystal. You know how people talk in a small town. And you know how you are when you've had a few drinks too many, Chrystal. I know it's quite normal for a woman to be interested in sex, my dear, but you can be so indiscriminate."

And she'd had to ask what indiscriminate meant! When Deirdre told her, she'd lost her temper again but Deirdre didn't turn a hair. "As long as you are under my roof, Chrystal, you will behave like a lady. I shall see that you have neither funds nor transportation and should you manage some other way, I shall send Tony after you."

Well, she had tried once. She'd hitched a ride with the boy who delivered groceries and she'd peddled her fur jacket to a woman at a thrift shop for twenty-five dollars. ("Twenty-five bucks! But it's sheared beaver." "I know, but beaver isn't in demand now and the jacket is dated, I mean that collar and those cuffs. Still, one of the college students we get in the summer might like it. They wear anything these days. But I doubt if it will bring much more than twenty-five dollars so that's the best I can do.")

She took the money and found herself the gayest-looking bar in town—it was early in the spring and the tourists hadn't come yet so this bar wasn't crowded but the best she could do, some of them weren't even open yet that time of year.

Well, she'd gotten into conversation with the bartender and a guy who had lobster pots ("Really? Boy, do I go for lobsters but they're so expensive . . .") but before she and Joe, the lobster pot man, could get out of there in came Tony Nero looking big as a house.

"Come on, Chrystal," he'd said and Joe asked her, quick-like, "Who's that?"

"I'm her husband," Tony Nero told him, grabbing her arm.

"He's not my husband, don't you believe him!"

But Joe slid off the stool like it was greased and mumbled something about his lobster pots needed tending and everybody else just looked away as though she and Tony weren't there at all.

She did a lot of cussing and some crying on the way back. Tony didn't say anything until he'd pulled up in front of the house and then, "Listen, Chrystal, you go along with Deirdre. It's the best thing to do, take my word for it. She's got the brains and the rest of us are dopes, don't know enough to come in out of the rain." He pulled out cigarettes and matches, lit a match and stared at it for a long minute like he'd forgotten what he lit it for. Then he touched it to the cigarette and said, "So you do what she tells you and you'll be the happier for it. You'll see."

Chrystal stubbed out her cigarette in irritation. She was doing what Deirdre told her, but damn it, she sure wasn't happy.

She picked the pen up. "I'm getting tired, Timmy, so must sign off. You know, it's a funny thing, but as I look back on everything it seems to me the worst thing that happened to me was when you died. We might have gotten married and had kids and all, you know. 'Cause you were the first guy I ever loved and if you hadn't been killed in an accident, things might have been different. I figure I still love you, you big ape. Chrystal."

Chrystal joined the work crew right after breakfast. Lindsay was in the library looking mournful as she composed a shopping list. She had to put the call into the grocery store before noon.

Forrestor was out mowing the piece of lawn around the patio and porch, Chrystal saw him through the dining-room windows. The Hinkle boys were waxing the kitchen floor, she could hear the cook Florida, a large woman with a voice to match, complaining that they were holding her work up. "I got to start getting lunch for this mob."

Clive was in the theatre, rerolling film, putting the canisters back in order. Tony came up from the cellar with a tool box, said he was going to fix a loose screen in Chrystal's room. "Thanks," she said absent-mindedly.

Deirdre, as usual, was nowhere to be seen. She never had breakfast with them, slept late. "While her slaves do the work," Chrystal muttered. She'd awakened with a headache. She'd had bad dreams.

Chrystal came out of the living room, dustcloth, lemon oil, and glass cleaner in hand, to find tiny Helena struggling with the suddenly big canister vacuum. She was running the vacuum over the bottom steps of the staircase, had to stop when the girl Cheryl came down.

"Excuse me," the girl said coldly. Stuck-up little thing, Chrystal thought, wondered what connection she had with Deirdre. This friend of Deirdre's, the girl's mother, was someone she'd never heard of. But then, there'd been many years in which she'd never laid eyes on Deirdre.

Helena said good morning, moved aside for the girl to go by. "Helena," said Chrystal, "that thing's too big for you to wrassle . . ."

"Where is everybody?" asked Cheryl.

"Doing our chores." Chrystal held out her cleaning wares. "I'm afraid you missed breakfast."

Helena pulled the vacuum away from the stairs, began to clean around the front door.

"I don't eat breakfast." Cheryl was wearing an ice blue linen dress, looked expensive to Chrystal. Too plain, though. "But I would like some coffee."

Helena looked up, brow wrinkled. "Gee, I don't know—the Hinkles are waxing the kitchen floor."

"Helena, give me that thing . . ." Chrystal hated vacuuming, but Helena just couldn't manage it, she went to take it from her.

"Where does that door go?"

Chrystal looked where Cheryl pointed. "It leads to the tower. This house was a church once, or part of it. Some kooky congregation ran out of dough before they got the church finished, that's what Deirdre told me. That's how comes it's got a tower." She handed the cleaning cloths to Helena. "If you want to do something, dust. That's more your size."

"I was just trying to help." Helena looked hurt.

"And I appreciate it, believe me . . . hey, Cheryl, don't go in there."

Cheryl, hand on the knob of the tower door, raised her eyebrows. "Why shouldn't I go in there?"

"Oh, nobody goes in there." Chrystal wasn't sure why she was making a point of saying no, but the girl acted so snotty, she just felt like bucking her. "It's all full of dust and cobwebs and maybe, like the Garson boy said, bats."

Cheryl gave a look that went under the heading of looks that could kill and twisted the knob. Chrystal was thinking of a nasty reply, the nastier the better, so she wasn't looking inside the tower way which was why, when Cheryl suddenly let out a shriek, she jumped and dropped the vacuum hose on Helena's foot which made Helena squeal.

Cheryl screamed again, an odd scream, Chrystal thought, long and thin, almost rehearsed. She went up behind her and looked in. There was something, someone lying on the floor in the middle of the tower hall. Part of the tower ladder lay on top of him. He was very still. Dust, caused by air coming through the open door, swirled. Chrystal sneezed and then said thickly, "My God. My God, who is it?"

Chief Griffin was a heavy-set man with thick gray hair and tired eyes. He'd come with the doctor, brought a policeman in uniform along with him. While the doctor went into the tower room and stayed there, the chief came back into the main house and told Chrystal and Helena that everybody should gather where he could talk to them.

"Everybody?" she'd asked stupidly. She couldn't think straight. Her headache and—now this. A terrible accident. Another terrible accident.

He gave her a sharp look, maybe he wasn't as worn out as he looked, and said, "Everybody."

She went to get Tony and told him, told him to tell Deirdre. Let him do it, she didn't want the job.

His eyes got like glass marbles but he didn't say anything, just nodded and went off. Chrystal went back to the living room where Helena, or somebody, had collected the rest of the household, even Florida and Betsy.

Cheryl was lying stretched out on the sofa, her face white as a sheet, sleeping beauty in a farce.

Helena was weeping, quietly in a corner, like a child. Chrystal sat clutching the cleaning cloth, it gave her something to hold onto.

"You found him, young lady, is that it?" Chief Griffin spoke to Cheryl.

She closed her eyes. "I opened the door . . ." Her voice was weak. "And saw him lying there . . ."

"Did you move him?"

"I couldn't . . . I just stood there, rooted."

Chrystal spoke up. "I turned him over." She swallowed. "I had to see if there was anything we could do. But—there wasn't."

"What's happened? Tony said there'd been an accident . . ." Deirdre appeared in the doorway, elegantly clad in something Oriental-looking, pink and gold. Tony looked in over her shoulder.

"Evan Garson," Chrystal told her. "He tried to climb the ladder to the tower and fell."

74

"Good God!" Deirdre looked appalled. "Is he badly . . . ?"

"I'm afraid he's dead, Miss Dunn." Chief Griffin gestured toward an empty chair. "Would you kindly sit down?"

"I warned him!" Deirdre looked to the others for corroboration. "I told him it wasn't safe."

"Yes." "She sure did." "She told him." The Hinkle brothers spoke almost simultaneously. Gene tugged at his bushy hair. They were huddled together, looked nothing like comedians.

Deirdre sat and Clive took up a protective position behind her chair. Florida, looking put upon, twisted a long wooden spoon between her fingers. The maid Betsy stared at the floor. The police chief didn't say anything, only studied them. The uniformed policeman, Chrystal thought fleetingly that he was a good-looking young man, had a notebook and pencil in his hands, was poised to write. Somebody was breathing hard. Chrystal, surprised, realized she was the heavy breather. She tried to calm herself. The body had looked so—broken.

"All right, one at a time," Chief Griffin said finally. "For the record. Starting with you, miss."

Cheryl opened her eyes. Chrystal saw the fear in them. Cheryl gave her name, lowered her lashes and waited. Part of a movie. Scene, the interrogation.

How did Cheryl happen to find the body?

Wide eyes once more at the word body. "I don't really know, an impulse. I came downstairs—the door was directly across the hall. I hadn't noticed it before, I was curious. Somebody told me it led to the tower."

"Somebody?"

Cheryl glanced around. "Chrystal. And Helena. Those two."

"I was getting ready to vacuum." Chrystal's hands tightened on the dustcloth. It was a piece of an old terrycloth towel. "Helena had the vacuum cleaner, we were cleaning the hall. I told Cheryl not to go in . . ."

"Why did you tell her that?" Even though the chief looked and sounded tired, his questions came quick.

"Deirdre didn't like us to."

"Is that so?" He didn't look at Deirdre, but she fielded the implied question.

"I didn't tell anyone it was forbidden . . . I just didn't want anyone using the ladder. It was rickety."

"Then why didn't you keep the door locked?"

Her lips tightened, eased. "We're adults. I don't like locked doors."

He looked directly at her then, but didn't speak.

"I don't understand this." Deirdre stood up. "Heaven knows, this is a terrible tragedy. A ghastly accident. But—police? I don't understand."

Chief Griffin's shoulders slumped even more. "This isn't the first accident at Belfry House." He sounded apologetic. Deirdre could do that to people.

Helena sniffled loudly. Forrestor handed her a handkerchief.

"Not the first? You mean—you mean the drownings? But they had nothing to do with Belfry House. Not actually. An immigrant gardener, unfamiliar with the area, the tides, very sad but understandable. And the Jenks girl. She wasn't quite bright, you know. Besides, she didn't work here. She had, for a couple of days, but I had to let her go." Deirdre sighed.

"Anyway, we have to look into accidental deaths." The chief tucked his chin into his collar. "It's the law."

"Is it? Yes, I suppose I know that. It makes sense, of course. You came around the other times. But now you sounded so . . ." She laughed ruefully. "I'm just upset. Forgive me. I didn't really know the young man, he came unannounced and uninvited, I should have sent him away. I guess I'm feeling guilty."

"Here's the doctor," Tony said from the doorway.

Chief Griffin walked slowly out into the hall, conferred, said, so they could hear, "The cruiser's on its way. They were way down on Route 3." He turned back to face them. "It looks as though he died from the fall, all right. Broke his neck."

"Oh," Helena wailed. And Deirdre said softly, "Poor young man."

"Anyone see him go through that door?" Chief Griffin straightened, Chrystal could imagine he'd told himself, "Shape up, you've got work to do."

Nobody, it seemed, had seen Evan since the night before. They told about that.

"There was a broken flashlight near him," the chief spoke to no one in particular. Then, "I'd like to look at his room, his belongings."

"Oh, yes." Deirdre came forward. "I'll take you. His things —I don't even know his address." Her dark eyes grew darker. "Whom do we notify? Who does that?"

"I'll take care of it," the chief told her. He beckoned to the officer who closed his notebook.

"You will? Oh, thank you. But I feel as though I should write his people, say something." Deirdre bowed her braided head. "I shouldn't blame myself, perhaps, but I can't help feeling responsible."

The chief gave her that searching look again. Chrystal got the idea that he didn't quite know how to handle Deirdre. Well, a lot of other people felt that way, too. "I'll see that you get the address," he said at last.

"And flowers," she thought aloud. "I'll want to send flowers. This way, Chief Griffin. I'm afraid there are two flights of stairs . . ." They moved out into the hall, disappeared, the uniformed policeman and Tony going with them.

No one spoke. Helena sniffled. Florida stalked across the room and out into the hall, heading for her kitchen. After a minute, Betsy followed, nearly running.

"He was such a nice young man," Helena quavered.

"He was such a fool." Cheryl sat up, brushed her hair back from her pale face.

Chrystal had had it with her. "You're some sweet kid, aren't you?" She made her exit on that one, paying no heed to Cheryl's hasty explanation that she'd meant Evan had been foolish because he wouldn't listen to Deirdre. She passed the doctor waiting for the cruiser to take the body. The door to the tower entrance was shut, thank God. She headed for her room, if there was one thing she didn't need, it was to see them carry his body out.

She skipped lunch, no appetite, and listened for the others to come upstairs. When the time was ripe, she went to Deirdre's room and knocked on her door.

"Who is it?"

Chrystal told her.

"I was about to have a nap. All right, Chrystal. Come in."

Deirdre, hair loose and hanging down her back, sat in the middle of the big bed, the emerald drapes that hung behind it formed a canopy at its head and accented the paleness of her hair and skin. Deirdre had something white all over her face, a *crème* of some sort that made a mask. Her dark eyes glittered more brightly than usual because of the contrast. Chrystal remembered their very first meeting. She'd been a chorus girl in a chintzy club, Deirdre was working as a hat check girl. "I'm going to be a great actress," Deirdre had assured her new acquaintance. "I know I'm no beauty, but you don't have to be a beauty and besides, I've got these strange eyes."

"Well?" the now Deirdre asked sharply.

Chrystal smiled. "I thought I'd go into town this afternoon. I'd like to use a car and I'll need some money." She'd already gotten dressed, wore a fairly new pants suit with a boxy jacket and big patch pockets, one of her last purchases before the bubble had popped and she'd come to live with Deirdre.

78

Deirdre scowled. The white mask drew little lines around the eyes. "I thought I'd made myself clear . . ."

"Oh, you have. But I won't be getting into any trouble. I'll just poke around in a couple of shops and later I'll drop into a bar and have a couple of drinks. I'll be home before midnight, no sweat." Her smile widened. She hadn't felt so sure of herself in months.

"Chrystal, you're such a child." Deirdre slid down on her pillows, closed her eyes. "I'm afraid the answer is still no."

Chrystal laughed gaily. "A child? At my age? Come off it, Deirdre. So what if I get hung up? It's my problem, isn't it? Nobody appointed you my keeper."

The dark eyes became slits. "You live in my house."

"Sure. And damned grateful, too. But I figure I pay my way. Let's see, the going wages for another maid would be . . ."

"If you don't like it, you can always leave." Deirdre's voice was hard.

"Oh, I know that. I've thought about it, but I'm still too young for Social Security and I don't figure anybody'd be too anxious to give me a job, so how would I live? No, I'll stay here and earn my keep, but I do intend to get a few fringe benefits. Like a day off at least once a week, everybody's entitled to that." She thrust her hands in her pockets. Silly hands, they'd started shaking.

Deirdre shut her eyes once more. "You think that's why I let you stay here? As an unpaid servant?"

"No, not exactly. But we all run our tails off for you, you can't deny that."

Deirdre's mouth set, cracked new lines in the facial mask. "I'm afraid, as I said before, the answer is no."

Chrystal's temper flared. "You know what you act like? One of those dictators. Or a warden in the lock-up. What gives you the right? I swear, Deirdre, even after all the years I've known you, I'll never understand you."

"Just take my word for it. I'm thinking of you. It wouldn't be wise."

"Well, wise or not, that's how it's going to be." Slowly she withdrew her hands from her pockets. "If you'll open your eyes, you'll see why."

Deirdre's eyes did open, also slowly, stared at Chrystal's open right hand. "What—is that?"

Chrystal came closer, but not too close. "You must have your contacts out. It's a piece of a ladder, see? A little section of a ladder rung. Here, at this end, it's broken off from where it fitted into the upright but here, at this end, it looks like it's been sawed through, doesn't it? Nice and smooth. Doesn't it look like somebody took a saw and cut it through?"

"Let me see that!" Deirdre reached, a cat snatch, grabbed the section of rung, looked closely at it. "Where did you get this?"

"When I turned the kid over, it was lying under him. I had a cleaning rag in my hand, I dropped it over it quick and carried it away with me."

"I'd better keep it." Deirdre's eyes dared Chrystal to take it back.

"Sure. Somebody might get the wrong idea. There's another piece, too. The other end, pretty much like this one. It wouldn't be so good if the cops got it, they might begin to wonder why somebody sawed the ladder rung. I wonder that myself, Deirdre. Seems like a funny thing to do to a ladder that nobody uses anyway. Have you got any idea who would do such a crazy thing?"

"How would I know? It could have been done years ago, the cut doesn't look new. Before I bought this place, somebody could have started some repairs and never finished them. How would I know?"

Chrystal nodded thoughtfully. "That's possible, because it sure doesn't make much sense, does it? But I figured if the cops found it, they might think otherwise so I picked it up." She paused for effect. "And the other piece, too."

"The other piece? Where is it?"

Airily, "Oh, I've got it put away. Where nobody will find it. You needn't worry."

Deirdre slid down on her pillows again. "I see. That's very thoughtful of you, Chrystal. And very clever."

She grinned. "Yes. Isn't it? Now, about the car and the cash . . ."

"You'll find some money in that carved box on top of the desk there. Not much, I don't keep much cash around. Will fifty dollars do?"

"For this week, I'll stretch it. If I think I'll need more next week, like if I find some clothes I'd like to buy—or have you got charge accounts?"

"No. Take what's there. I'll get a check cashed before next week." Deirdre's eyes drooped, her breathing was even. She seemed on the verge of going to sleep.

"All righty." Chrystal opened the carved box, took out the bills inside and counted them. "Fifty-three dollars," she announced. "I'll leave the three bucks. In case you need some change."

"What time do you want to go?"

"Oh, say an hour from now? I've got to fix my face." She laughed. "It takes longer these days."

"Forrestor can drive you."

"I don't need Forrestor to drive me, don't want him. I can drive myself. I've got a driver's license."

"All right, Chrystal. Whatever you say. I'll tell him to bring the Pinto around to the front door in an hour. Anything else?" Was she watching from beneath her eyelids?

"No, I guess that should do it. I'll try to be home by midnight like I said, Cinderella! But if I'm not, expect me when you see me."

No answer. Chrystal hesitated, then went to the door.

Deirdre's voice came sleepily. "Be careful, Chrystal. You be careful."

"You bet your sweet life." And outside in the hall, she did a little dance step. She had the handle now, oh baby, she had the handle now!

Hypsignathus monstrosus—*the enormous, peculiar muzzle and lips (with capacious cheek pouches) may be used for manipulating juicy fruit. Adult males produce bell-like "kwoks" every second throughout the night. To attract females?*

Forrestor . . .

Forrestor was reading a book and feeling somewhat guilty. He should be writing to his daughter, he'd had her last letter for over a week now. But writing to his daughter was not a task he relished and the book he was reading, or rereading to be more exact, for the third time, was his favorite, *Lolita*.

Still—if he didn't answer Sonja's letter, she would begin to get nervous and telephone like she did the last time. And the one thing more difficult than answering Sonja's letters was answering Sonja in person. So he sighed, put down his book, picked a caramel out of the bagful by his chair, and chewing, mouth happy, good thing he still had his teeth, he loved caramels, fetched his box of stationery.

Sonja's letter lay inside it. He arranged the box so he could write on its top, took a pencil from his shirt pocket so as to be ready, and opened Sonja's letter. There were questions in it that he must answer. If he didn't—ring, ring, the telephone.

"Dear Father," Sonja had written, "I don't know why it is that I must always begin my letters by begging for mail. Don't you know how much I worry about you, or don't you care?"

He licked the end of the pencil, wrote carefully, his handwriting wasn't as good as it once was. "Dear Daughter, I am sorry I haven't written, it's just that we've been so busy— the times we have! Of course I know that you worry about me and of course I care. I'll try to do better."

Back to Sonja's letter, second paragraph: "How is your health? Have you been taking your pills? You know what the doctor said about your heart. Is the arthritis in your knees any better? Have you done as I suggested and found a good doctor there, just in case? At your age, Father, you cannot neglect your health."

He wrote: "I'm feeling fine. Really quite good. I am taking my pills and I do believe the arthritis has eased considerably. Most of the time I'm so busy that I don't have time to think about it and that's half the battle, ha-ha."

He tried to think, what was the name of that doctor who'd come with the police to look at the poor Garson lad? Cheeney? Chesney? Something like that. He'd have to do, Deirdre had a thing about doctors. "The less you think about your aches and pains, the fewer you'll have," was her creed. "Stay away from doctors and think good thoughts."

"I have contacted a Dr. Chesney here," he wrote, "he comes highly recommended" (that was no lie, if the police used him he must be a pretty good doctor) "and, if need be, I can call him. But, happily, I feel no need at this time. Yes, I know at my age I must take care of myself and I do. Eight hours sleep each night and a nap at noon, plenty of good food."

Sonja asked: "How many people are staying there now?

86

Is Lindsay Ball still there? And that Nero fellow? And that other one, I simply cannot remember her name, it's simply too fantastic. Chrystal something? I cannot understand why Miss Dunn collects all these people. I realize that I have never understood theatrical people even though my own father was involved in the business all his life. But then, you were seldom home if you remember. Mother and I, rest her soul, had to shift entirely for ourselves."

"Yes," Forrestor answered, "Lindsay and Tony and Chrystal are still here and so are the Hinkle brothers, you've probably seen them, the Three Cuckoos? And Clive Keith, and Helena Edwards, a dear old friend has arrived recently with a young woman named Cheryl Harris who is the daughter of an old friend of Deirdre's. We are all most compatible and enjoy each other's company because we have so much in common. As I have often told you, I sincerely am sorry that I was away so much when you were a little girl, but I had to make a living. For your mother and you."

When he'd written that, he stared at it, wondering whether he'd put it too strong. No, damn it, he hadn't. His wife Pansy (who'd named their daughter Sonja Victoria, speaking of fantastic names) had hated his work and, he thought, ended up hating him. He should have married somebody in the business, that's what he should have done. It might have made all the difference, all those lonely days and nights . . .

Back to Sonja's letter. "Nonetheless, I feel a great responsibility for you and Harold and I have always been willing to make a home for you, you know that. You could live with us, we have a spare room, you don't have to live on charity which is what it seems to me when a perfect stranger takes you in out of pity."

He had to be careful with this part of his reply. "I know you and Harold would welcome me in your home, but, as you pointed out, I have been in the theatre all my life and my habits are quite different from yours and Harold's. I simply feel that I would be too much of a burden and I don't want to be that. As for Deirdre, I have known her for many years, from the days when she was a young, aspiring actress and I do believe I was able to do her several kindnesses at the time for which, she tells me, she is eternally grateful."

He put the pencil down and took another caramel. The sweet stickiness permeated his mouth. What a woman, Deirdre Dunn. What a wonderful, understanding, forgiving woman. Because of her attitude, he was able to look back on their early acquaintance without shame. She'd been very young, said she was eighteen but looked more like sixteen, all bones and those big eyes. It was her first job, she said, her first stage job and she was thrilled. Thrilled! All dressed up in black satin that made her arms and legs look like sticks as she pranced around on stage in a parody of the sexy accomplice of Sandor the Magician. Sandor, who was a big hulk named Dave Sanborn and who was also a terrible magician.

So he'd felt sorry for the kid and he'd asked her out to dinner a couple of times, "Got to put some meat on those bones, my dear," and then, the third time . . . he just couldn't help it. He'd felt so sorry for her, he just wanted to pet her a little, comfort her, poor little skinny kid, and that ape Sandor broke in on them there in the rooming house and took it all the wrong way.

But Deirdre had stood up for him. Black eyes blazing, she'd yelled at Sandor, "You have no right to talk, you bastard!" And Forrestor remembered that he'd been a little shocked that she knew such a word.

Well, Sandor had given her the ax, of course, fired her on the spot and Forrestor had gone to bat for the kid, called his agent, in those days he'd had a good agent, and talked him into taking Deirdre on. Whereupon she'd hugged him and told him she'd never forget him and, bless her heart, she never had.

The only thing was, and this disturbed him, she'd gotten the wrong idea about him somewhere. Could it have been the then agent, Corky Boynton? Just because he'd had to call on Cork for help a couple of times? Nah, Corky wasn't that kind of a guy. Even if he had dropped Forrestor McMann from his client list a few years later. "Baby, you're not worth the trouble."

But somehow Deirdre had found out about the girls in the movies. She'd brought it up right after she'd invited him to Belfry House.

She'd said, "Forrestor, dear, let's get one thing straight. You're welcome to stay here as long as you like, more than welcome. But there'll be no incidents. Do you understand me? No young ladies in dark movie theatres. And the best way to make sure of that is for you to stay right here. You can see all the films you want to in our own theatre."

He'd blinked at her. "I don't know what you mean."

"Yes, you do, sweetie."

He shook his head stubbornly.

"All right." She was sitting at her desk in the library and she pulled a sheet of paper from a stack, wrote briefly on it, passed it across to him. "Do these names mean anything to you?"

He read and his old heart leaped painfully, he could still remember the shame, the acid taste of shame in the mouth. Still remembering, he reached for another caramel.

"They were mistaken, those children," he'd insisted that day to Deirdre. "Once, I leaned over to find something I'd dropped and I touched her knee by accident. And the other times . . ."

"Forrestor, Forrestor." She'd sighed and smiled. "I know from experience how tender young things affect you. We'll say no more about it. Just stay on here at Belfry House with the rest of us old folks. We'll get along just fine." And she'd smiled at him, that dazzling, still dazzling Deirdre smile and they had said no more about it. But sometimes, his heart got lonely . . .

Back to Sonja's letter.

"But you have no regard for kith and kin, you never have had, so I don't expect you to change now. You say you are banking your Social Security checks, that you don't need money. For your own sake, just in case, heaven forbid, anything should happen, I urge you to change the account to a joint one, adding my name so that we could avoid all that ugly red tape in the event that, God help us, you should fail suddenly.

"Please do this immediately, Father. It is for your own good in case you should need money for medical care or funeral expenses. As you know, all Harold's free cash is tied up in his business and times haven't been too good and an emergency would find us in financial difficulties.

"So make it a joint account right away, Father. The bank will send me a little card and I will sign it and send it back and if I don't get this little card in a few days, Father, I will know that you . . ."

He made a face and wrote a final paragraph. "I have not been able to get to the bank as yet, Daughter, Deirdre takes care of it for me, banks by mail, but as soon as I can I shall change my savings account to a joint one as you suggested.

"Summing up, I am well and happy. With fondest affection to you and Harold, your Father."

He read the letter over, folded it and put it in its envelope. He was just addressing it when the knock at his door came.

"Yes?"

"Mr. McMann, Miss Deirdre says for you to take the Pinto round to the front door."

Forrestor went to the door, opened it, looked out at Betsy who wore her usual sullen expression. Didn't the woman ever smile? What sorrow had she had in her lifetime?

"Thank you," he said. When Deirdre had learned that he enjoyed fooling with the automobiles, shining them, tuning their motors occasionally, she'd given him the title of Keeper of the Garage. She trusted him with the keys, knowing that he wouldn't go off when he'd promised . . . "Is Miss Deirdre going somewhere?"

"She said it was for Miss Chrystal."

"Oh, I see. Perhaps she'll mail my letter for me." Odd, he thought, stamping the envelope from a small book of stamps he kept in the stationery box. Deirdre never let any of them use the cars except Tony. An unusual occurrence. He wondered if Chrystal were going to Truro and, if she were, sudden thought, maybe he could ride in with her. It had been months since he'd been out of Belfry House and surely Deirdre wouldn't mind if he just rode along. A pleasant little spin would be the ticket. He wouldn't even get out of the car.

"Sorry," said Chrystal when he asked her. She almost pushed him aside to get into the driver's seat.

"But . . ."

"Here, give me the letter. I'll mail it. I can't take you with me, Forrestor, because I don't know when I'll be back." She turned the key in the ignition, made the engine race much too fast.

Absurdly disappointed, he hadn't realized how much he yearned for the bustle of a main street, he handed over the envelope and stepped back. The Pinto roared off, almost flying down the driveway.

Dejected, Forrestor walked back onto the porch, was startled to hear someone say, "What on earth was that?"

It was the new girl, Cheryl, looking out through the screen door. "Chrystal is going into town," he told her.

"Not if she drives that way, she isn't." Cheryl stepped back so he could come in. She was wearing a beach robe and carrying a towel.

"You're going bathing?" he asked. He was grateful for someone to talk to. He didn't care at all for this naptime routine, made him feel like a child.

"Yes, if not swimming at least some sun." She placed dark glasses over her eyes. "There's nothing else to do."

"Would you care for some company?"

The dark glasses stared at him. "I'd like some company. Very much."

"If you'll just wait until I change—and get my book. It's pleasant to read by the sea."

"I'll wait out on the side porch, where we were last night."

"I'll hurry." Forrestor was pleased. A young person could be stimulating. Just as well that Chrystal had said no after all. He got into his swim trunks and a shirt, brought a towel and *Lolita*. At the last moment, he thought of the caramels and brought those, too.

Cheryl was waiting as she said she'd be. They walked down the steps, across the patio and through the dunes. His sunglasses snapped onto his regular glasses. He flipped them down, offered Cheryl a caramel.

"No, thanks. You're an old friend of Deirdre's, huh?"

"Yes. Yes, indeed. Must be close to half a century since we met."

"Fifty years. That's a long time."

"Well, to tell the truth it isn't quite fifty, more like forty or so. I'll confess that fifty is such a good round number, I fibbed a little. But forty at least, yes, a bit over."

"She must have been pretty young."

"Yes, a mere child."

"Did you know her family?"

He should have taken his shoes off, they were quite full of sand. "Her family? No, I never met her parents. Now that I think back, she never mentioned them. I always had the idea that she was an orphan or that she'd run away." He stopped. "If you'll wait just a moment . . ." Standing on one foot, he tried to slip out of a shoe.

"Here. Lean on me."

He put his hand on her firm young shoulder. There, one shoe, two shoes. He laughed happily and picked them up. With the caramels, book, shoes, and towel he had quite an armful. The sun felt good, very good.

"I didn't mean her parents," said Cheryl when they'd reached the beach and set up beach chairs. She started to take off her robe. She was wearing a very brief swim suit. He looked away, squinted into the sun. "I mean her husband and child."

Surprised, he looked back to her. She was a slim young creature, like a faun. "But—didn't you know? Tony Nero is Deirdre's husband."

She yanked off the dark glasses and stared at him. "Tony Nero?"

"Why, yes. For ever so long. She kept her name, of course . . ."

"But they don't act married."

"But, my dear, they are. They've been married for, well, I hate to be repetitive, but almost forty years."

"Then—" She stopped short, put the sunglasses back on, turned to face the sea. "They had children? At least one child?"

"A little girl. Leila. Deirdre thought the sun rose and set in that child."

"Did she?" Her voice was peculiarly sharp. "I can't picture her as the motherly type."

"Well, she was." Forrestor leaned back, popped a caramel into his cheek. "I didn't see them often, you understand, but occasionally our paths would cross. Leila was always with her, Deirdre took her everywhere."

"How sweet." He couldn't make out her tone. It sounded —almost bitter.

"A beautiful little girl. Eyes like her mother's, only not so dark. And a face like an angel. A little blonde like you, no, lighter blonde, I should say. And masses of ringlets. Enchanting." He bit into the caramel, recalled, "I was quite cross at Deirdre because she didn't invite me to the wedding. She wrote a lovely letter, though, explaining that it was a family affair, very small. And then, after that . . ." He lowered his voice, "Came the tragedy."

"She was killed, you mean."

"Yes. She and her young husband. I never knew him. But Deirdre . . . I telephoned long distance the moment I heard, Deirdre was in California at the time and I was so concerned about her. I knew how highly she regarded the child. I was afraid that she would be utterly inconsolable."

"Was she?"

"Deirdre is a very strong woman. She suffered, of course, but she suffered inside. She threw herself right into her work, made three pictures in a row and then she moved here." He swallowed the remains of the caramel. "That was her swan song, those three films. She retired from the business."

"Over twenty years ago."

"Yes, it would be just about that. But the public hasn't forgotten her. The things she did were so memorable."

"Yes, I've seen some of them at least four times on television. I wonder why she had only one child."

"Oh, I'm afraid I can't answer that." Why had he and Pansy had only one child? Well, he could answer that!

Cheryl stretched, arms high, stomach in, chest out. Forrestor reached for his book, opened it.

"I've got to be careful of the sun," she smiled. She had a very sweet smile. "Would you put some of this oil on my back?"

Forrestor cleared his throat, closed his book. "Yes, of course." He took the bottle from her and she rolled over on her stomach. Her shoulder blades stuck out like a little girl's.

Awkwardly, he began to smooth the oil on. It was hot, he was perspiring.

"Why do you stay here?"

He paused in his massaging. "Why—because I enjoy it. Deirdre asked me to."

"Don't you have any family? Are you all alone?" Her voice was sympathetic, perfect for the part. Nice young lady, being kind. He basked in the warmth.

"I have a daughter. She lives in Rye, New York. She's asked me to stay with her but, I don't know. I don't want to be in the way. And the others—well, the Hinkle boys had a few wives between them, but they're all divorced now and no children. They've got another brother in Los Angeles who didn't like show business, he went into real estate. I guess he's done well, too, but I don't think they get along if you know what I mean."

"And Lindsay? Chrystal? Mr. Keith?"

"I believe Lindsay has two sisters, older than she. I'm not sure where they are, though. Chrystal? She's never said. And Clive's mother and father are still living. Imagine that! They're in a rest home in Florida. That's where all his money went. He told me he had to buy their rooms, it was that sort of deal. So many thousand dollars and they could stay there the rest of their lives. It broke him, but he did it." He'd run out of space on the broad of her slim back. He started to put the top back on the bottle.

"That was nice of him."

"Oh, Clive's a very good sort of fellow. A little too good, I suspect. Sometimes this business is dog eat dog. Clive often got eaten."

"Put some oil on the back of my legs, too, will you please? What about Helena?"

Slowly, he took the screw top off the bottle again, poured liquid into his hand. Her thighs were rounded, pale, a little girl's thighs attached to a little girl's bottom . . . "Helena

95

is all alone. She lost her parents and her young brother many years ago in a fire. Terrible thing." Very carefully, he placed his hand on her leg, ran the hand down to her knee, so soft, her skin so smooth. Little tingles in his fingers, did she feel them, too? Now, apply the oil up higher, at the edge of the brief bathing suit where the flesh rounded abruptly . . .

Cheryl turned quickly and sat upright. "You dirty old man!" Her pretty blue eyes were now narrow slits, her soft pink lips hard and tight.

"I beg your pardon? I'm sorry . . ." Forrestor's face was scarlet, he could feel his cheeks burn.

Coldly, very coldly, he could feel the sudden chill, she turned her back to him, got up and walked away to the sea. She waded in and, as soon as she could, disappeared beneath the water.

He didn't know what to do. To stay—or to go. To apologize abjectly, or to pretend nothing had happened, that it had all been a mistake, his hand had merely slipped. Which it had, yes, damn it. Looking at it in one way, it had.

He prayed she wouldn't tell Deirdre. But she wouldn't, why would she tell Deirdre—a lie? Yes, that's what it amounted to. He hadn't done anything, not really, he'd actually controlled himself very well. Hadn't he? Yes, he had.

Biting his lip, he walked to the water's edge. She was floating, now paddling in the water, waiting to catch a wave. "I believe I'll go in now," he called. "I'm truly sorry if I offended you. I didn't mean to—my hand slipped."

She stood up, she was in water breast deep, and looked back at him. The sun was in his eyes, he couldn't be sure that she looked at him with such hatred. "When I get back to the house," she said, voice clear, bell-like, a young girl's positive voice, "I shall tell my grandmother about you."

"Your—grandmother?"

"Yes. Deirdre Dunn is my grandmother. You didn't know that, did you?"

The sound of the surf was loud in his ears, crashing waves, some other sea, not the one that sparkled there in the sun, blurred his vision.

She was Deirdre's granddaughter. She would go to Deirdre, she would tell her that he had . . . Deirdre's face came fuzzily into view, her voice through the roaring, "Not another time, Forrestor. Not one little slip. If you do, you will have to leave Belfry House. It's as simple as that."

He bolted then, ran across the beach, across the dunes toward the house. His heart was pounding, he shouldn't run, it wasn't good for his heart, his tired old heart, but the thought of life with Sonja pursued him. Hell. Damnation. Punishment. He couldn't bear it, he couldn't, he'd rather be dead and in a box!

He stopped at the porch, unable to continue. Sweat was dripping down his face, clouded his glasses, it was hard to breath. He leaned against a pillar and wished the last half hour away. Why? Why had he gone with the girl to the beach in the first place? She had encouraged him. Yes, she had by being kind, with smiles and sympathy. But he'd spoiled that, she would tell Deirdre, he knew that, remembered or imagined the cold fury in her blue eyes.

He would tell Deirdre first. He would tell her how it happened. "Nothing at all really, a slip of the hand, that oil is greasy, that's all. I swear, Deirdre!"

He began to breathe more easily. He pulled his shirttail up to wipe his face, used a corner of it to wipe his glasses. He must find Deirdre now. She would be in the gym, perhaps, or in her room. He hoped she would be in her room, alone, not with Tony in the gym . . . he hurried to the gymnasium door, pushed it open even as he knocked on it.

The room was empty.

The hall was empty, too, the rooms abutting were empty. He wanted to run up the stairs (get it over with) but he forced himself to go slowly, quietly. Please, Deirdre, please

97

. . . despite his efforts, he was out of breath again when he reached Deirdre's door.

He stopped, listened. Silence. So many people but such a big house, how quiet it could be. As though they were ghosts. He tapped gently on the door, whispered, "Deirdre?"

No response.

He rapped harder, spoke louder, and the door, barely latched it must have been, swung open at his rapping. He looked in, words of apology ready. There was an expanse of green carpet and a huge green and blue bed with green curtains hanging like a canopy at its head. But the big bed was empty. He stepped inside, said, "Deirdre?" He thought he heard something down the hall, someone coming? He closed the door quickly. He must have been mistaken, all was silent.

Deirdre was not in her room. The door to her private bathroom was open, she wasn't in there either.

Where was she? He had to find her before the girl did.

He looked around for a clue, somebody, something had to help him. He'd never been in Deirdre's room before, hadn't thought what it might be like. There was a personality to the room, but was it Deirdre's? Peculiar thought. Yet, it was somehow a cold room for all its blue and green and white brightness. A disciplined room, brushes, and bottles and such placed just so on a white marble-topped bureau. No disorder, none at all.

Where could she be?

He thought he heard footsteps in the hall again. Deirdre! She could be coming to her room. He turned eagerly and then realized where he was, what he had done. He was in Deirdre's room, he had entered uninvited like a thief. She wouldn't like that. Oh, no, she wouldn't like that at all.

He panicked and looked for a place to hide. Behind the green canopy, behind the bed. He slipped behind the draperies, heart hurting in his fear, and, instead of a blank white wall as he had expected, he found a door.

A door? Hidden behind Deirdre's bed? Where would it lead? Why should there be a door hidden behind Deirdre's bed?

Someone came into the room.

Phyllonycteris asphlla, *the Jamaican flower bat, thought to be extinct is not. Flower bats eat some tropical fruits in captivity, but are unable to break the skin of a large fruit and so must search for a spot where the fruit has been injured before it can dine.*

Lindsay . . .

Lindsay was, of course, sorry
that the young man had died, but she was disappointed
mostly because the funeral would be held elsewhere. There
was a ritual about a good funeral that held her spellbound,
satisfied some sense of important theatre. A good funeral,
thought Lindsay, was more moving than a play because it
was, after all, real.

She didn't get to funerals often any more because Deirdre
made it difficult for any of them to go into town. But she had
been to two funerals since she'd come to Belfry House, that of
the gardener who'd drowned and then that of the maid who'd
drowned, too. On both occasions, she'd said to Deirdre,
"Don't you think someone should represent Belfry House
at the funeral?" and Deirdre had said she supposed so and
Lindsay had volunteered to go. She had an excellent costume
for funerals, long and black with a small veiled hat.

The gardener's funeral, not very impressive, he had, after

all, been a foreigner and probably didn't know many people. His wife had been there, the widow dressed in all black with a black shawl over her head, and there was a priest, of course, and a handful of his fellow countrymen who lived in the area, and Lindsay. Other than the funeral home people, that was all. Very sad. It was well that she went.

On the other hand, the services for the maid drew a large crowd. Her father and mother, lean-faced New England prototypes, sat in stoic silence amid the townspeople. From conversations overheard, Lindsay knew that the girl had been born and reared in the town, had been "subject to fits" at an early age and had, in the words of one woman, "Lived a tragic, short life. Poor Cecilia. Perhaps it's a blessing."

The minister had pulled out all the stops in his eulogy, "A lovely blossom plucked too soon," etc., and there were snifflings throughout the church. But still, the father and mother sat, outwardly emotionless. Or, if not emotionless, then angry. Lindsay got the impression from the set of their backs that they were angry. For what reason, she wasn't sure. Because of the bathos? Or because unkind fate had taken a life? Or, maybe they were angry because they had to raise and care for the girl. There were people like that, Lindsay thought.

Well, these were two interesting memories, but now she'd be unable to go to Evan Garson's funeral. Too, too bad. He'd been rather charming. She could have, she thought, summoned some genuine emotion at his last rites.

She had the instructions for her own funeral written out in detail. She'd told Deirdre and Deirdre had given her one of those Deirdre-looks and said, "Dear, morbid Lindsay. I couldn't possibly write out a thing like that. But then, I never intend to die."

Joking, of course, but that was all right for Deirdre, only it wasn't Lindsay's way. She would be cremated and then what was left of Lindsay Ball would be divided into two urns, equally, of course, and sent to each of her sisters. Whether she wished this because she loved or hated them, and she did both love and hate them, she wasn't sure. But the urns would be pretty, she'd described their design in her instructions, and would look well on the mantel, or wherever. Lindsay rather fancied a mantel, but one of her sisters, Della, lived in a trailer home and Lindsay doubted that she'd have a mantel. Perhaps on top of the television? She'd add that possibility to her instruction list.

But not now. She had to go over to the servants' wing and speak to Florida now. Deirdre had complained that Lindsay's menus had gotten unimaginative. "I can tell the day of the week by the main course and vice versa," was the way she had put it.

"But you didn't care for the frogs legs and I can't think of anything different," Lindsay had answered. "I told you when you gave me this job that I wouldn't be any good at it. Food just doesn't mean that much to me."

"Well, it does to me. Talk to Florida. Surely the two of you can come up with something. I can't abide another meat-loaf-on-Monday, pork chops-on-Tuesday. Do something to earn your keep, Lindsay."

The last remark shouldn't have hurt, it was true enough, but it did. "I don't have to live here, you know. You need me more than I need you." She'd regretted that, instantly. She'd gone almost too far, come too close to a subject they never, never discussed. A subject that Lindsay, one of the few qualified to discuss, had even trained herself to never think about. She'd braced herself for the expected reaction.

But it hadn't come. Deirdre merely looked away and, after a moment, said, "Please talk to Florida. I'd appreciate it, Lindsay. I get so little pleasure . . ." Her voice trailed off and Lindsay said quickly, "I'll try. I'll really try."

So now she must try. Florida had about as much imagination as a goat; in fact, she had the disposition of a goat.

But then, she'd been with Deirdre for umpteen years as had Betsy. That was the way it was at Belfry House, only old associations need apply. Lindsay left her room to go to Florida's. She had her hand on the doorknob of the cross wing before she realized she'd have to go the long way around. The police had locked that door after the accident, taken the keys.

Accident? Well, of course, accident!

And there was another topic now to add to the list of topics definitely not to be talked about. How many taboos did that make? Too, too many. Better to think about funerals. Everybody would have to be buried—someday.

Lindsay went down the hall to the empty kitchen, stopped to draw a glass of water. It was a warm day, very warm. Drinking the water, she glanced out into the hall to see Forrestor, face red and glistening from the heat, go down the hall to the stairs. He didn't see her. She reminded herself to tell him that his musical saw was missing from the living room. Had he taken it away for some reason, or had someone else borrowed it? What would one borrow a musical saw for? To saw something? Why not use the regular saw in the tool box? And what needed sawing, anyway?

Rungs in a ladder?

Stop that! She turned the empty glass upside down by the sink and went through the back passage, knocked on Florida's door.

She heard a squeaking of springs and then the cook's voice, sounding sleepy, "Who's that?"

Too bad, she thought, I've awakened her from her nap. She'll be in a temper. "Lindsay," she spoke lightly. "Deirdre asked me to speak to you."

More springs squeaking, then heavy footsteps coming toward the door. "It's my rest time." The door swung open and Florida filled the aperture. She was wearing a light robe of many colors, a sight to behold.

"I'm sorry, but Deirdre said . . ."

"Are you coming in? 'Cause I'm going back to lying down. My feet are killing me."

"Of course." Lindsay seated herself in a cane-bottomed chair. It was a small room but the furnishings were nice. Deirdre was generous to those who stayed by her. "It's about the menus. Deirdre wants us to think of something new."

Florida, putting herself on the bed, grunted. "Pheasant under glass, I reckon."

"Well, yes, I suppose . . . can you do them? Of course you can, you're a marvelous cook." A little sugar never hurt.

"Where'm I gonna get pheasants? That little store that delivers don't carry no pheasants, you know that." Florida frowned. When Florida frowned, her whole being seemed to join in.

"I don't really think she means that we should do the impossible. Just more variety. It's the spice of life, you know." She smiled but Florida glowered harder. "Chinese food, perhaps. How would that be?"

"Italian's easier." Said grudgingly.

Lindsay was relieved. "That would be different. And perhaps we could do other countries, too. German and French, the French have so many ways to fix things. I'm sure you'd be good at it."

"Oh, I know how. But it isn't my place to say anything. She says you're the one to tell me what to cook. If you want me to, I'll figure out something for next week."

Absurdly grateful, Lindsay smiled again. "Wonderful. I'll leave it to you." She should have spoken to Florida long ago, it seemed. Communication. A very good thing.

"What about the other meals?" Florida asked suddenly. Lindsay, startled, looked at her. Was there a calculating expression on that broad face? What did Deirdre pay Florida to be her faithful servant? Enough? Lindsay had always imagined she paid her plenty. But how much was enough?

"Aren't they the same?" Lindsay got up from her chair, ready to go, through with communicating with Florida. Florida didn't know the rules, or, if she did, she wasn't following them.

"I guess so. Most of the time. Okay. I'll see what I can do. I'll bring you a list so's you can order."

"Thank you." One last glance. Florida's expression was bland. She yawned widely. "Get back to your nap," Lindsay told her. "I'm sorry I interrupted it."

"I'm due it, you know. Work from early morning to night."

"I know. I don't think we could manage without you." And, closing the door behind her, Lindsay thought, faithful and devoted servant. Yes, she had been, she'd been that. What else could one ask for? Under the circumstances?

At dinner, they were minus two. Chrystal, said Deirdre, had gone into town for the evening and Forrestor wasn't feeling well. "Tell Florida to save some soup," Deirdre told Betsy, "and I'll take it up to him after dinner."

Cheryl made a tiny, snorting sound, continued to eat her bouillon.

"Is it anything serious?" asked Helena, small face concerned.

"No, I'm sure not. Just a stomach upset. He'll come around in a day or two. What shall we do this evening? There are nine of us, too bad. We could play some bridge, but that leaves someone out . . ." Deirdre didn't ask for volunteers to be left out, but she got one.

"I don't care about playing," Lindsay said. "I'm a little tired tonight, I think I'll go to bed early."

"Well, if you're sure . . ." Deirdre was pleased with her, Lindsay knew. But not surprised. If not Lindsay, it would have been one of the others. They knew their lines. "Tony, will you set up two tables after dinner?"

Tony, chewing stolidly, nodded. As was also expected. Lindsay could remember when he hadn't been so docile. But the years—and sorrow—had a way of taking the fight out of some people. What, she wondered, did those two talk about when they were alone? Or, did they talk about anything? All right, all right, get off that subject. Her mind was misbehaving. What it needed was a good funeral to keep it occupied.

She finished her dinner quickly and asked Deirdre if she couldn't take the soup to Forrestor. "I'm going up anyway."

"That would be sweet, Lindsay." Deirdre flashed a smile, continued her conversation with Cheryl. She was telling her the history of Belfry House and the countryside. "I've been told they'd planned for bells in the belfry, but the whole project was so ambitious for a small congregation and they ran out of money . . ." When Betsy brought the tray with soup to Lindsay, Deirdre broke off again to say, "If he doesn't answer, do go in. He might be sleeping, but he must have some nourishment."

And that's what Lindsay did because Forrestor didn't answer her knock. She said, "Forrestor," and when he didn't answer, shifted the tray to one hand and found the light switch with the other. He was lying on his side, face averted, so she put the tray down on the dresser top and walked around the bed, saying, "Forrestor, I've brought some soup. It will taste good. Forrestor . . ."

She carried the tray carefully back down the stairs, stopped at the living-room door where they were just starting their bridge game, and announced, "I'm afraid Forrestor is dead, Deirdre. I think he's had a heart attack."

And she was thinking, poor little man, we'll give him a lovely funeral.

Atrozous Pallidus, *the pallid bats, eat flying insects and terrestrial anthropoids, even scorpions. Although the scorpion has a venom which can be lethal, the pallid bat will attack. It is not known whether the pallid bat is immune to the venom or simply better at in-fighting.*

Abner Kitchener . . .

Abner Kitchener took off his uniform cap and hung it on a hook on the coat rack. He rubbed his forehead where the cap had left a mark, since he'd grown his hair fuller the darned cap was too small for him.

He stopped by the water bubbler and drew a cup of water, drank it down before going into Chief Griffin's office. The chief was sitting in front of an electric fan, talking on the telephone.

"No, Mr. Harding, I didn't tell her that Evan Garson was out of your department. I didn't know whether to tell her or not and I figured if I didn't, I could tell her later, but if I did, I couldn't not tell her if I shouldn't have."

Abner cast his eyes heavenward and tried to stand in front of the fan, too, to let the breeze cool his fevered brow. He'd read that someplace, it sounded good.

"Well, Dr. Chesney is doing a post-mortem, but he says it looks to him like a simple case of Garson falling and breaking his neck." The chief reached into his middle drawer with a free hand, dug out a cigar, put it in his mouth and rolled it around. Abner found a match and lit the cigar for him.

"Sure, I locked the place up. Both sides, though one of them was locked anyway. Took the keys with me. We'll go over it with a fine-tooth comb, like you say, but we already looked once and all we found was a lot of splinters, some hunks of broken wood, some dust, and a few spiders."

Whoever he was talking to, a Mr. Harding, talked at length while Griffin listened, puffed on the cigar. How could he smoke a big cigar on a hot night like this, Abner wondered.

"No, he didn't get in touch with me at all, but the way I understand it is he just got here the day it happened. I mean, he didn't get much of a chance to contact me, did he? Only, the way I figure it, it would have been much smarter if he had of. Don't like to talk about the dead, but this fella of yours must have been one of those eccentrics. Playing at detecting. Detecting's nothing to fool around with." He rolled his eyes at Abner.

Abner pulled up a walnut chair and sat down near the chief so he could share the breeze from the fan. Chief Griffin, having listened, spoke again, "Well, you can send somebody else down here if you want to, but I don't see what good it will do if the fella fell and killed himself. Miss Dunn warned him, everybody agreed that she did. You can't arrest her for having a rickety ladder in her house, at least I don't think you can. Sue her, maybe, but not arrest her." He flashed a triumphant look at Abner, a look that said, I've got him there, all right.

More talk from the other end with the chief smoking and nodding his head, then, "Sure. I'll let you know the minute I know anything more. You've told his dad, you say? Fine. You'd better let me have the address. Miss Dunn said she wanted to send some flowers. And tell the kid's father to let us know where to send the body when we get through with it."

And then he said, "Oh?" and, "Is that right?", and, "Okay, I'll play Mickey the Mope," and "All right," and "Goodbye," he hung up, heaved a sigh and looked at Abner. "That man's sure got a hair across his lip."

"Was that the Attorney General's office in Boston?" Griffin had moved so that he was getting most of the air from the fan, Abner hitched his chair closer.

"Fella named Jim Harding. Special assistant. I wanted to tell him the thing was plain foolish to start with. Some young guy playing cops and robbers. Sure, there could have been something funny about Cecilia's drowning. And maybe even the Portuguese. But that's no way to go about investigating, sounds more like one of those crazy spy things that nobody believes anyway. If I had the manpower and the time, I'd look into the background of all those old nuts at Belfry House, that's what I'd do."

"Why don't this Harding do that? They've got the time and men."

"That's what I told him. Said he had. And I said, so what did you find out? And he said, nothing to tie them to nothing. Most of 'em lived like Arabs anyway, moving from pillar to post. When the Portuguese died there was only five of them there, Miss Dunn and that Nero guy, he's her husband, did you know that? And that weird-o in the goofy clothes, Lindsay Ball, she was there then, along with the cook and the maid. A little later on that Clive Keith dude showed up and then the strip-tease dancer joined the party and the little old man that plays music, he calls it, on bicycle pumps and such. They were there when Cecilia died, and Harding says he's still waiting for word from California because the little old guy, McMann, lived in a bunch of spots there but it was some time back; it's hard to trace 'em all and the Clandestine woman, that's not her real name of course, hung her hat at so many places it might take years to get all the reports." The chief ran out of breath, puffed his cheeks out at the fan. "It's a mighty hot night. Looks like a long summer."

"I reckon there's no law that says they couldn't have all three been accidents." Abner longed to unfasten his shirt collar, but the chief wouldn't go for it.

"'Course there's no law. Only those book writers say things like that. Law of averages, coincidence, that stuff. Truth is, some places like some people are just losers. At least, that's the way I see it. Now, where there's ocean, you're bound to find drownings. And that Belfry House, it's an old place, bound to be rickety in spots. Throw in a bunch of damn' fool people and anything can happen." The fan scattered ashes across the desk top.

"Still"—another thing Abner would have done if he'd been alone, he would have put his feet up on the desk—"you did do some investigating. Because of Cecilia."

"Hell, Abner, how'd you like her papa on your neck? For one thing, he's a past Selectman and for another thing he's a big Bible man, eye for an eye and a tooth for a tooth. He's got it in his mind that something funny's going on out at Belfry House and he wants to smoke the sinners out. But, as far as I can tell, ain't none of them breaking any laws."

"What's Harding want you to do?"

"Didn't you hear me? Go over the accident scene with a fine-tooth comb. Keep at 'em until something or someone cracks. He talks like that. Reckon he feels guilty for letting the boy come down here on that harebrained scheme. His father's some big scientist, famous, with dough, you know? He's probably raising a big stink in Harding's office. So they say froggy and expect me to jump. Damn it to hell"—he slammed his hand down on the desk—"I've got a town to take care of. Can't waste all my time on a bunch of weird-os."

"That Miss Dunn, she's lived out there a long time, hasn't

she?" Abner had just finished his supper and had to cover a belch.

"On and off for over twenty years. And that's another thing. No trouble at all until the last few. So if anybody's gone off his rocker, it's got to be one of the Johnny-Come-Latelys. She's been a fine, upstanding taxpayer, so far as I know. Good-looking woman, even today. And always sends in a nice check for the boys on the force at Christmas. Bet you didn't know that."

Abner looked at the chief sideways. He seemed in a pretty good mood, usually wasn't so confiding. "That young girl out there, she's a pretty one."

The chief chuckled. "I saw you throwing sheep's eyes but I didn't see her catching. What's the matter, Abner, losing your touch? I hear tell you're the Don Juan of Truro on your time off." The amused expression disappeared and he leaned forward. "And it sure as hell better be on your time off."

Abner grinned. "You know better than that. I got ambitions. You don't get anywhere if you let your social life interfere with your ambitions. As for that girl at Belfry House, maybe you didn't see it, but she gave me the once over, all right." His grin widened. He knew his thirty-inch waist made his shoulders look broader than they were, which was pretty broad to begin with and the fact that he had black curly hair and a dimple in his chin wasn't exactly a kick in the ass.

The chief humphed. "If I could spare you, I'd send you out there to waltz her around, see if you could find out anything."

"I wouldn't mind that."

"I know you wouldn't, but I can't spare you. I've been here too long for one day myself and you get your tail out of here and ride that cruiser. A hot night's the only excuse some idiots need to run a Jaguar up a telephone pole."

Abner repressed a sigh. He would miss the fan, but when the cruiser got going with its windows open, it wouldn't be

117

so bad. On the way out he retrieved his hat, drank another cup of water. Burke, at the desk, was about to make some crack, had his big mouth open, when the phone rang.

"Truro Police Station. Officer Burke speaking."

Abner finished the water, threw the cup in the waste basket.

"Yeah, Doc, the chief's here. Hold on . . ." He pushed a button to switch the call to Chief Griffin, said to Abner, "There's another one out at Belfry House."

Abner, hat in hand, felt his mouth drop open. "You're kidding. Who?"

"Somebody named McMann. That was Dr. Chesney, he's out there now. Says he thought the chief would want to know even though it looks like a heart attack."

Abner whistled softly through his teeth. Coincidence? Some places are just plain unlucky? Maybe—but maybe not. In the humble opinion of Abner Kitchener, humble opinion, hell; in the opinion of Abner Kitchener, maybe not.

He waited for the chief to emerge and when he did, face grim, he said, "Want me to go out to Belfry House with you?"

Chief Griffin, pulling car keys out of his pocket, all but snarled, "I told you—go jockey that cruiser."

And Abner went.

Which was why he was the one who first arrived at the scene of the accident. A Pinto, flipped onto its hood like some giant insect upended. The car had obviously come into violent contact with, not a telephone pole as the chief had predicted, but a tree, a large oak that stood the impact much better than the car. Abner figured the car had smacked the tree, skidded off, hit a ditch the wrong way and overended. He had to guess that was what had happened because there was no one to tell him.

The occupants of the car, two of them, were quite dead.

One was Sam, the bartender at the Calico Cuckoo, Abner wasn't sure of his last name. The other was a red-haired woman later identified as Chrystal Clandestine.

118

And the boys from the garage who towed the wreck in said the line holding the brake fluid had been partially sawed through. Not all the way, just enough to make it drip, drip, drip till it was all gone.

Coincidence? No way.

Chilonatalus, *among the smallest bats and smallest mammals known. Attractive little creatures, they are small enough to hide in a pants cuff or under a shirt collar.*

Helena . . .

It was that song that triggered it. Evan Garson had sung that song and for a moment she'd thought he was singing it to her. That horrible song about doing relatives in! She hadn't slept well that night, nor any night since. The dreams had come again, and it had been a long time since the dreams had deviled her. Now, returning, they seemed so much worse than before. She wondered if they could drive her mad.

But that night, the night he had sung the song, she had awakened, mouth open, ready to shriek, and stopped herself just in time. And heard someone in the hall. Did they move like someone sneaking, hiding, or did she just imagine that because of the dream? Heart beating hard, she slipped out of bed and went to the door, bare feet making no sound on the carpet. She cracked the door and peered out.

Giant shadow moving toward the stairs, shadow cast by the small lights spaced along the wall. Male shadow, dressed in dark colors. There a moment, then growing smaller, more in proportion, then gone. She wasn't sure who it was. No, she wasn't, couldn't be sure. It must have been Evan going to the tower entrance. Must have been!

Now, night again and a second death, Forrestor. Helena sat rigidly in a chair by her bedroom window. Sat on a pillow so she could see through the window. Dark out. They had taken Forrestor's body away. Deirdre had called his daughter, reported to them all in surprised tones that the daughter had seemed more furious than sad. And they had spoken of their memories of Forrestor for a little while. Helena had cried, found as usual some solace in the crying. Then they had drifted off to their rooms and she had wanted to beg someone, anyone, to stay and talk with her but, of course, she didn't.

So she sat there, afraid to sleep and so weary.

She should leave this house.

But where would she go?

She'd given up her little apartment. Shabby sort of apartment, low rent, but still it had been home and such places were hard to find. One of her neighbors, Edna Klinger, had told Helena that her, Edna's, sister had been put out of her place, they were tearing the building down, and all Edna's sister had been able to find was an efficiency at the absurd rent of $150 a month before utilities.

It had seemed such a blessing when Deirdre had invited her here. But this was an unlucky house. She had the gift— or curse—of feeling such things, had even sensed it when they drove up to the door, but she'd told herself not to be silly. An overactive imagination, that was her trouble. That's what she told herself.

She yawned involuntarily and her eyes drooped. So tired, so in need of rest, sleep, blessed sleep. But they waited there, in the darkness . . .

Think about Deirdre. How dreadful she must feel. All her goodness twisted by ill fortune. Not her fault that Evan had fallen and died, not her fault that Forrestor's heart had stopped.

Helena's head felt so heavy, she forced it up, widened her eyes, but they wanted to close, would close, no matter . . . Tony Nero, dressed in black, was tiptoeing down the hall, coming toward her, singing softly, "About a maid I'll sing a song who didn't have her family long, not only did she do them wrong, she did everyone of them in, she did everyone of them in . . ."

And there was young Helena, so long ago, fifteen and eight months of age but as small as a six-year-old, smaller than some. And looking at the world through hate-filled eyes. "Why me? Why? Why? Mother, Father, even Jimmy, all the proper size. Why me?"

Her mother, tight-lipped, quoted the Good Book and said it was the will of God. Her father said nothing, he never did. But she felt the shame he felt, she knew that in his heart he wanted to hide her, lock her in the attic. Which they did sometimes when she was particularly bad. And she could be bad, very, very, very bad. To Jimmy, for instance, James Elgin Edwards, Jr., aged twelve and already five foot six. "She weighed her brother down with stones and sent him off to Davy Jones . . . one day when she had nothing to do, she cut her baby brother in two . . ."

No, wept the aged, sleeping Helena, I didn't do those things. Little cruel things, yes, but not those awful things.

No, said Tony Nero dressed in black with a robot's face, but you made a candle of wax from melted crayons and used a piece of string for a long wick and that last time when they let you out of the attic, you left the long wick smoldering toward the candle hidden under the eaves, hidden in a box of baby clothes, Jimmy's baby clothes, and in the middle of the dark night you smelled the smoke and you thought you'd wait until just the right moment, then you'd save their lives and they'd be grateful, so grateful, wonderful Helena!

So you waited until the smoke came and began to burn your eyes and then you went out into the hall and, dear God, the hall was filled with smoke, filled full with it! You coughed and choked and cried tears that had nothing to do with sorrow then and you went to your mother and father's door and pounded on it, screamed, coughed, screamed, "Fire! Fire!"

But they didn't answer and they always kept their door locked, why did they lock their bedroom door? Frightened now, truly frightened, panic-stricken you went to Jimmy's room and burst in, he was lying there so still in the midst of a smoke-filled square, a square formed by four walls and somebody was pouring smoke into the square although no more would go. He wouldn't answer, wouldn't respond, so you ran from the house and the smoke followed you out the door and the flames crackled over your head, found exits through attic windows and places where there were no windows and you screamed and screamed and screamed . . .

Someone screamed and Helena awoke, listened. Silence. No, not silence. A telephone ringing somewhere. A telephone screaming. She pushed herself out of her chair, hurried to the door, a dark shadow passed down the hall. "Tony?" whispered Helena.

He turned. His face in shadow, she couldn't see the features. "The phone," he said and went down the stairs.

Helena followed, heard him answer, heard him say, "Yes. Yes. No! But how . . . My God. My God. Yes, I'll tell . . . Now? They're all asleep. I see. All right. All right." And when he hung up and came up the stairs again, there was a most peculiar expression on his face. And he said, "Chrystal has been killed in an accident. The police are on their way here now. I'll awaken Deirdre. You start knocking on doors, Helena. We've got to get everybody up. They want to talk to all of us."

126

Walking the second-floor hallway, she smelled smoke in her nostrils and began to cough.

Chief Griffin came with two uniformed men, one's face was familiar, he'd been there before. Kitchener and Tinkham, their names were, the chief said. Or, so Helena thought he'd said. She'd been crying when he made the announcement but not so loud as not to hear. Officer Kitchener would take someone into Truro to identify the body, the chief said, and Deirdre, ashen-faced, replied that Tony would go. Tony went to get dressed. He'd been wearing a dark blue bathrobe over pajamas.

"I knew I shouldn't let her take the car, I just knew it." Deirdre spoke rapidly, words spilling out. "Where—how did it happen? Was she alone? Had she been drinking? That's a foolish question, of course she had . . ."

Helena peeked through her handkerchief at Deirdre. It wasn't like her to babble like that. She looked odd, as well. Eyes glittering, face distorted. The face she could control so well. But why not, three deaths in—was it only three days? Unlucky house, jinxed house. Helena's eyes teared up again. She must leave. Tomorrow.

"Yes, she'd been drinking. And she was with a bartender from the Calico Cuckoo, by name of Bly, Sam Bly. He was killed, too." Helena thought the chief was watching them in a most peculiar manner.

"She was a speed demon," Cheryl Harris spoke up. "I saw her drive away, she almost flew out of the driveway."

"Is that so?" Helena lowered her handkerchief to look at the chief. He sounded different, quite different from the way he had sounded earlier. Almost—excited. What did the young people call it? Up tight? "Well, you may be right," he went on, "she may have been a reckless driver. Maybe she wouldn't have lost control when the brakes went if she'd been an expert operator. It depends, of course, on how fast she was going and how sober she was . . ."

"When the brakes went?" asked Deirdre sharply.

"That's right. That's bound to happen when there's a nick in the fluid line." The chief looked around the room. "Where's the rest of you?"

"Forrestor McMann passed away this afternoon." Deirdre's voice was low.

"I know that. I mean the big woman, the cook, and the other one, the maid. I want them here, too."

Deirdre looked puzzled. "But why? They knew Chrystal, of course, but they were hardly friends . . ."

"Somebody want to go with Tinkham here to get them?" He cut Deirdre off brusquely.

"I'll show you," Clive Keith volunteered. "We'll have to go the back passage, you've got the front one locked."

"Chief Griffin"—Deirdre used her commanding tone, it seemed to Helena she was back in control now—"you're behaving . . . what exactly do you want from us? This is a house of sorrow. Two friends in one day—and that poor young man. Three acts of God, if you will. His finger is pointing at Belfry House. But that hardly calls for . . ."

"Miss Dunn"—the chief hitched his trousers up—"somebody here thinks we're pretty small potatoes and I suspect you share the same opinion. Well, I suppose we are kind of backwoods cops. Not up on all the smart capers. But some things are clear as a horseshoe in a plate of hash. And a sawed-through brakeline is a sawed-through brakeline to anybody that takes the trouble to look."

"Sawed?" "Brakeline?" "Through?" The Hinkle brothers went through their act, not at all funny and not meant to be.

"I see." Deirdre pushed her shoulders back, sat tall. "You are implying that someone here—I assume here—contributed to Chrystal's accident. But why one of us? Aren't there vandals all over the world who delight in doing such senseless things? Surely Truro isn't immune."

The chief nodded vigorously. "Could be. Sure, could be. But you see, when you add four and one it comes to five. There was the Portugee and the Jenks girl and then along comes the Garson fella and the old man and now Miss Clandestine. All accidents—or natural causes? Right? Until Barney Gates, he works down at the garage, took a look at the car. New Pinto, you see, and Barney likes Pintos. Maybe he thought it was a shame that a new car got busted up, maybe he figured this Ralph Nader's got something and he poked around to see if something defective caused the wreck, I don't know why he bothered, to tell you the truth, except that he does some work for us and maybe he's picked up a trick or two. Anyway, when one of those accidents looks like it wasn't an accident, gets us to wondering. And there's something else you don't know that makes me mighty interested in the folks at Belfry House."

Deirdre's dark brows rose.

"Evan Garson. He was with the Attorney General's office in Boston. Came here to check into those first two drownings."

Deirdre's mouth fell inelegantly open. "He was what?"

"I can see that comes as a big surprise, Miss Dunn, but it's a fact. Ever since he broke his neck, I've been pondering the question. He came here incognito, I guess you'd call it. Did somebody find out who he really was and do him in? If so, then there was something real wrong about those drownings. Only, I asked myself, how could anybody find out? Nothing in his gear to show it. 'Less somebody made off with some papers. But I don't figure there was anything. He was too set on the part he was playing for that, if I figure him right he left all his identifying stuff at home. So, next I wonder: Did somebody do him in for another reason? Or, was it just a plain and simple accident? One way or another, he was sticking his nose in someplace he shouldn't have been? That's the kind of questions that have been running through my mind ever since and I'll tell you, the answers don't come easy."

Deirdre smiled a Mona Lisa smile. "You have been busy. I swear to you that none of us had a single suspicion. I believed he was a rather simple but nice young man who was hooked on bats." She looked around. Everyone nodded vehemently.

Helena couldn't help adding, "I don't believe it about Evan."

"Oh, it's true all right. So, as I was saying, I might have done a lot of wondering and a little looking into corners and not much else, having no proof as it were. But things began to happen pretty fast. Take the McMann fella—Doc Chesney will look into that pretty close, now. Not that he wouldn't have in the first place, but it's one thing when you've got a little cause for suspicion and another when you've got a solid reason."

"Forrestor had a bad heart. His daughter will tell you that. I'll give you her address . . ."

Deirdre was interrupted this time by the arrival of Florida and Betsy, followed by Tinkham and Keith.

"I was sound asleep," Florida complained to Deirdre. "How'm I gonna get up to get breakfast if I can't get my sleep?"

"I'm sorry, Florida." Deirdre's tone was placating. "The chief insisted we awaken you. Do me a favor, Chief Griffin," she almost purred, "be kind to Florida and Betsy. I couldn't exist without them and they are certainly completely innocent. They hardly saw Evan Garson."

"Well, I'll tell you, Miss Dunn"—he made that hitching motion at his trousers again—"I'm inclined to agree with you, but I wouldn't be much of a police chief if I didn't ask them some questions. But, since I'm real interested in what you were telling me, you may have a point there. I could send Tinkham into the next room with them and let him get some questions and answers real quick. How would that suit you?"

The black eyes glittered. "I wouldn't like that. I want to be present. I won't have you intimidating them. I've read about . . ."

The chief smiled and Helena thought, he must have been nice looking when he was a young man. "Police brutality? Whatever you say, Miss Dunn. Sit down, ladies. I think breakfast might be a bit late in the morning anyway, so don't you worry too much. Now, as you were saying, Miss Dunn?"

Deirdre fiddled with the gold braid on her robe. She was wearing what Helena would have described as lounging pajamas with a short belted top. Rather fancy for sleeping, Helena thought, but then maybe she'd been sitting up reading, or something. "I'm afraid I've blown my lines, Chief Griffin." Her smile was shaky. "I need a prompter."

"McMann had a bad heart, you were saying." The chief smiled back, a friendly, almost admiring smile, it seemed to Helena. "Don't doubt that he had. But that gives me something else to ponder about. Most likely I would have thought the old boy just couldn't stand the excitement, kind of churns you up to find somebody dead in your house. Yes, I probably would have thought just that except for the fact that on the very same night Miss Chrystal Clandestine goes to her reward on account of a sawed-through—well, not sawed-through completely, only partially, just enough so it would take awhile for that brake fluid to leak out . . . but, I'll tell you the truth, Miss Dunn, it kind of boggles the mind when so much happens so quick."

"Chief, you look tired. You must be tired, it's so late. Why don't you sit down." Deirdre switched to the role of hostess without so much as shifting a gear.

The chief inclined his head politely. "I appreciate the offer, Miss Dunn, but the minute I sit down this time of night I tend to get drowsy. So I'll just stand if you don't mind. If it gets too much for me, I'll take a chair."

She nodded. Helena had the strangest feeling that the two of them were stage center and she and the others were a weary audience. "I understand. You're absolutely right, too. Perhaps I should stand, it will help me think better." She did and there was something about the way she stood that made her look very tall. "I've listened to what you have to say and I'll confess you make sense."

Lindsay, wrapped in something pink and ruffly, made a sudden movement by the fireplace. It was so abrupt a movement that every one looked. Except Deirdre.

Deirdre paced, eyes came back to her. Two steps forward, two steps back. "This is my house. I know these people. I have known these people for a very long time. On this basis, I shall take into consideration what you have told me and what I know. And I offer a postulate."

Gene Hinkle giggled nervously. "I thought a postulate was a young man."

Deirdre glanced his way and he subsided. "I put to you . . ." She was concentrating on the chief and he on her. They stood apart like dancers not dancing. "I put to you the proposition that Rojas and the Jenks girl did, indeed, drown accidentally. I put to you that Evan Garson did, in fact, fall accidentally from that rickety ladder about which I warned him. And then we come to Forrestor and Chrystal about whom, you say, you have the most doubts." She paused and Lindsay moved again. There seemed to be something uncomfortable about the long, frilly skirt of her robe. All those ruffles. Helena had never cared for ruffles. They made her feel shorter.

"You see . . ." Deirdre moved to the mantel, posed gracefully against it. "I know something about Forrestor McMann that you don't. When I tell you, you may wonder why I invited him here, but he was kind to me years ago and he was a sick old man, needing friends, needing care . . ."

Now it was Cheryl's turn to attract attention. She made a small sound, then said nothing.

What time is it? Helena wondered. She had left her watch on her night table. Was it too late—or too early? Up all night. Bats stayed up all night. That made her think of Evan. She was suddenly frightened. She didn't know why.

Deirdre changed her position, apparently deep in thought, finding words difficult. Still against the mantel, but a new pose. "Forrestor had something to be ashamed of, bitterly ashamed." Pause. "He was"—pause—"a child molestor." Someone exhaled. Cheryl?

"I knew it, I knew all about it." Deirdre spoke quickly now that the awful words had been spoken. "It doesn't matter how. When he came here, I told him, no more fun and games. He agreed. Any of us who knew him knew how he would re-act to public knowledge of this—shortcoming. Especially if his daughter knew. He was terrified of his daughter. Guilt complex, you see. She and her mother lived much of their lives on their own. He pretended that he left them so he could support them, but he did little of that. And I put it to you, Chrystal found out his secret."

"So?" The chief looked halfway asleep, but he was still on his feet.

"Chrystal was—I guess you could say greedy. She'd run through any money she'd earned. She was truly a charity case without a penny. Forrestor, on the other hand, had a little money. A bank account. I suggest that Chrystal learned his ugly secret and blackmailed him. I wondered where she got the money to go into town, even asked her but she only laughed and asked me back, 'What if I've got a sugar daddy?'"

"You're saying that the old man sawed the brakeline?" Chief Griffin looked thoughtful. Tired, but thoughtful.

"He could have, easily. He brought the Pinto around for her. He sometimes did little motor repairs, engines and auto-mobiles interested him. If he did cut the line, wouldn't it follow that the agitation, the guilt, the anticipation would be too much for him? Wouldn't that be logical?" Deirdre looked from one to the other. The Hinkles nodded, Cheryl agreed, Clive Keith murmured, "My God, how awful." Lindsay fooled with the ruffles on her robe. Helena felt like sobbing aloud but didn't, an act of will.

"Maybe so." The chief studied Tinkham who was writing things down. "Better go up and look around both rooms, Tinkham." To Deirdre: "Are they locked?"

"No. I told you we don't lock doors here. Betsy, show the officer Mr. McMann's and Miss Chrystal's rooms." The maid, with ill grace, led him out.

Helena thought, I don't believe it.

Lindsay, in the silence, said to Deirdre, "I want to call my sister. I'll reverse the charges."

"But, of course, Lindsay. Don't worry about the charge." Deirdre's smile was forced, Helena thought.

"If she'll have me, I'm going to stay with her." Lindsay and Deirdre might have been alone in the room.

"Oh, Lindsay . . ." Deirdre clasped her hands together. "Why? Why would you leave me?"

"I'm going, too," Helena blurted. "I'm frightened."

"We thought we would . . ." "Our brother in California." Two of the Hinkles let their sentences trail off, the third finished for them, "We can't stay either."

"Hold your horses, now," the chief told them. "Until this business is cleared up, you'll have to hang around."

"But how long?" Clive Keith wanted to know. "I was thinking of paying a visit to my parents. They haven't been feeling tip-top . . ."

Deirdre broke in, voice ragged. "All of you, leaving me? My friends, please don't . . ." Her voice broke and Helena felt ashamed but would go just the same. As soon as she could. Perhaps she could get her apartment back, it had been such a short time.

"I won't be leaving you." Cheryl Harris's words were emphatic.

Deirdre glanced at her. "Thank you," she said softly, her voice almost lost in the sound of footsteps coming down the hall. Officer Tinkham came in with the maid behind him. He had an envelope in his hand. "Found these in the lady's room," he told the chief. "In a jewelry box. Nothing else in it."

The chief took the envelope. "Box wasn't locked?"

"Nope. Had a lock on it, but it wasn't fastened. The box was hidden under a pile of stuff in the bureau."

Chief Griffin sighed, opened the envelope and brought out some papers, yellowed newspaper clippings it seemed. He glanced through them, looked up at Deirdre and said, "Looks like your idea could make some sense. These are about the old boy. Being arrested." He read on, silent for a few moments. "For molesting young girls in movie houses." He asked Tinkham, "What did they find in her pocketbook?"

"The usual stuff. And a little over twenty bucks in cash."

The chief narrowed his eyes at Deirdre. "Pretty cheap blackmail."

She shrugged. "Perhaps he didn't have much cash on hand. His bankbook must be in his room somewhere."

"I haven't been to his room yet," said Tinkham. "Thought you'd want to see these."

"Miss Deirdre, do I have to go up there again?" Betsy spoke abruptly. "I'm dead tired and I don't like standing around while he paws through their stuff." Her face was mutinous.

"If it's all right with the chief, I'll accompany the officer." Deirdre sounded weary, too. "Can't they go to bed?" she asked Chief Griffin.

The chief scowled. "Either of you see one or the other, Miss Clandestine or Mr. McMann, yesterday? See anything you think you should tell me about?"

"I didn't see nothing," said Florida flatly. "I was in the kitchen—or my room—all day."

"I didn't see *her*"—Betsy stressed the word her—"but I saw him. Going down toward the shore with that one." She indicated Cheryl, added as an afterthought, "One other thing. His saw is gone." She pointed to the corner. Forrestor's odd conglomerate of musical instruments brought tears to Helena's eyes.

"His saw?" asked the chief almost stupidly.

"His musical saw," Deirdre explained, said in sudden realization, "Oh!"

"What kind of a saw?"

"A regular one, but very shiny. He kept it polished."

Chief Griffin asked Cheryl, "You were with him yesterday?"

"For a while. He sat on the beach and I went swimming. He . . ." She licked her lips. "He made a pass at me."

"He did what?" Deirdre sounded appalled.

"I didn't know anything about his problem," Cheryl spoke defensively, "and I asked him to put some suntan oil on me and—he had wandering hands!" Her cheeks were scarlet.

"What did you do?" Chief Griffin was interested.

"I called him a dirty old man. I told him I was going to tell Deirdre."

"But you didn't."

"No. He seemed so scared and I couldn't help feeling sorry for him. I thought, he won't do that again. I thought I'd just stay away from him."

"Miss Deirdre . . ." Florida's tone was a whining one.

"All right," the chief nodded decisively, "go on to bed, the two of you. If I need you, I'll talk to you tomorrow. And Tinkham, you go back upstairs and see what you can find. Reckon you'd better check all the rooms. That all right with you, Miss Dunn?"

Deirdre looked taken aback. "All the rooms? But why?"

Helena saw a glitter in the chief's eyes. "Just to satisfy my conscience. You can stay with Tinkham while he looks around. No reason why he shouldn't, is there?"

"Why can't we all go up?" asked Gene Hinkle belligerently. "If anybody's going to search my place, I want to be there."

"All right, all right, we'll all go. Then nobody will have anything to complain about." The chief turned to lead the way.

"I'll stay here," Cheryl was positive. "I've got nothing to hide."

"Cheryl, my dear"—Deirdre assumed a cooing tone—"that's not the point. None of us have anything to hide."

Cheryl shrugged. "Let me know when I can go to bed."

I don't want to go to bed, thought Helena. I want to go to my room and pack. This ugly, ugly business . . . dear Forrestor, how could he be what they said he was . . . she didn't understand what was going on, but something terrible was happening. Something frightful had come to live in Belfry House. Going down the hall she shivered. She was too old to die . . . she'd lived just long enough to know that life was too precious, don't take it from me before my time . . . poor and sad and all alone, but she wanted to live, to live, something nice was due her, something nice . . . she wouldn't die in Belfry House!

Lasuirus cinereus, *the red and hoary bat, the most spectacular and beautiful bat in North America.*

Deirdre . . .

"Did he believe you?" asked Cheryl. She was stretched out on the living-room sofa, looking quite comfortable and wide awake, acting as though it were midday rather than well past three o'clock in the morning.

"I hope so." God, how absolutely weary she was. Tony had returned from town, yes, of course it was Chrystal, and, like the others had gone to bed when the chief left. That man could sleep like a cat, anywhere, anytime. Deirdre sometimes envied her husband.

"Did they find the saw?"

"Yes. In his room."

"Do they think he used it on the Pinto?"

"The chief said he'd study it. I suppose they can tell under a microscope or something."

Cheryl put her slippered feet on the floor, watched Deirdre in the mirror. "All the rats are leaving the sinking ship."

Deirdre didn't bother to argue with her phrasing. "Yes. I didn't expect that. But you'll stay, you said. That makes me very happy."

The girl's cheeks flushed, she looked away. "I got the idea that maybe you need me." Almost angrily she added, "At last." And then, "I don't understand why you stay in this place. You could go anywhere, do anything."

Staring into the mirror, the very depths of the mirror, Deirdre said, "I must stay put."

"It's your life, of course, but catering to all those hangers-on, just because you need companions . . . you could get one of those lovely condominiums they're building in the city, be in the center of things, go to the theatre, see people." She stopped, appeared to be thinking. Then, cautiously, "I'm sorry, maybe I'm talking out of line."

Deirdre guessed at Cheryl's sudden thought. That it might be money. Well, in a way she was right. Running this big house all these years had cost plenty. Florida and Betsy were certainly not inexpensive. Their kind of loyalty came high. But there was still enough to last, there had to be enough. Only—last until when? How long did the money have to last? That was the question that haunted her. The girl was looking at her curiously, she realized she'd been silent too long, spoke quickly, "I love it here. The privacy. And besides, I have company, my audience if you will, Tony. Tony is always here. And . . ." She turned, looked directly at Cheryl, "You said you'd stay. I count that as a promise."

"Do you want me to?" For the first time, the young face was vulnerable.

Deirdre went to her, held out her hands. "Indeed I do." Cheryl, hesitating, reached out, clung. "Then I will."

Deirdre went to Tony's bedroom, rapped softly on the door. "Are you asleep?" she asked quietly.

"No. Come in."

She entered. He was sitting, smoking, watching the first streaks of dawn. "Is everything all right?" she asked.

"Yes. I went up, just came down. The only question was: Where were you?"

"What did you say?"

"Sleeping."

She laced her hands together. "I'd better go see." She started for the door, turned, "Tony, Cheryl says she wants to stay here."

"What do you think?"

"I want her to stay. Very much."

"If she does, you'll have to tell her."

"Yes, I think I will have to."

He put out his cigarette with concentration. "Will you be able to trust her?"

Deirdre nibbled her lower lip. "I think so."

"Is that good enough?"

"It has to be good enough."

He turned his face to the window. "It's up to you. As usual."

Would they never think alike? Probably not, after all these years. They never had. It just made it so much harder to fight him and then fight all the other battles. "Lindsay is leaving. What about her?"

"Lindsay is leaving?" He was surprised and she remembered that he hadn't been there and so told him about the general exodus.

"I don't care about the others," he said. "Good riddance. But Lindsay knows. Maybe we'd better not let her go."

"Tony!" Her voice was too sharp, she quieted it. "You can't. Not again. If we get out of this, we're very lucky. We'll just have to chance it. We've looked ahead, planned for that sort of thing anyway. And she's been loyal, very loyal. I don't expect that will change. They're not angry, I don't think, not any of them. Just frightened."

"I don't like it. When is Lindsay leaving?"

"As soon as the police permit. I don't know, it seemed to go all right, I think Chief Griffin believed me. What did you do with the ladder wood? And the diary?"

"Burned them."

"You opened the lock on the jewelry box very nicely. They thought it had simply been left unlocked."

"I've learned to do some odd jobs for you, learned to do them well, wouldn't you say? Some very odd jobs." His voice was bitter.

"For yourself, too." How dare he blame her?

"The most foolish thing I ever did"—he swung around to look at her—"was to fall in love with you."

Oh, no, she thought. I can't stand one of his moods. Not tonight. "I'll go along," she said. She started for the door.

"When are you going to tell the girl?"

"Why do you always refer to her as the girl? She's our granddaughter. She's Leila's child."

"Because to me she's a stranger." He glared. "Everyone's a stranger."

"I'll tell her when the others leave." She took two more steps to the door. "They took the saw away. Do you think you handled it well?"

Wearily, "Of course. McMann fingerprints and, I trust, some faint traces of brakeline in the teeth."

Doubts loomed. "I do hope they're clever enough to find them."

An elaborate shrug. "We've done everything but draw them a diagram."

"Poor Forrestor." She squared her shoulders. "But, when it all got out of hand, it had to be somebody."

"Yes." That was one thing they agreed upon. Somebody —but not Deirdre. And not Tony. Except if it had come to that . . .

"Good night, Tony."

He didn't answer, only looked away and stared out at the dawn, fiddled with a pack of matches he held in his hand.

Had they then, in that single moment, been thinking alike?

"Thank you, Betsy." Deirdre reached for her coffee cup and leaned back, sipping. She and Cheryl, sitting in the shade on the porch, had finished their luncheon which had been served by Betsy with a certain amount of grace, for a change. Pleased, no doubt, that her work load was so much lighter. Now that the others had gone.

"I'm so lazy," Cheryl slumped in her chair. The girl seemed more cheerful, too, Deirdre thought. Was now a good time to set the stage? Deirdre imagined that it was. So, plunge in. Do it.

"Would you like me to tell you about your mother?" asked Deirdre.

Cheryl sat up, said she thought she'd switch to the chaise longue and did so. "My mother and father. Alvin and Leila Sechrest. That's my name and I can't get used to it. I've been confused ever since I read Alice's letter. Should I use the name Sechrest? Not Harris?"

"Legally, I suppose so. Otherwise, what does it matter? She was a beautiful child, your mother . . . "

"Yes, I know. Golden curls, lighter than my hair color, a mass of ringlets."

"Who told you about your mother?"

"Forrestor McMann. The day we went to the beach."

"Well, his description, though a bit florid, was accurate. She had a strange life, poor darling. Pillar to post with Mama, the film star. You don't know how much I regret that. She missed so many things, a house that was truly home, friends who would be friends over the years, a sense of belonging." She saw Tony, inside, coming toward the porch, waved him off when she found that Cheryl had her eyes closed. He arched his eyebrows and she nodded. He disappeared.

"I know I'm repeating myself," Deirdre went on smoothly, "but that's what I wanted for you."

Cheryl's eyelids flickered. "But you were here. Almost all those years. I could have stayed here."

"I wasn't here all the time, not when you were a baby. And by then, you'd already been settled with Alice. I had to go on with it." She leaned forward. "And besides, there was another reason."

The blue eyes opened wide, stared into her brown ones.

Now that we're at the nitty gritty, thought Deirdre, why do I find it so hard? "Your mother was the other reason," she said quickly and simply.

"My mother? I don't understand. My mother was dead."

Play the part to the hilt now, a shake of the head. "No. The woman in the car with Alvin Sechrest was not your mother. It was some stranger, some prostitute I'd guess. We never did know, never tried to find out. We simply identified the body as that of your mother."

Cheryl sat, very tall, very straight. "You did what?"

"Tony and I. We identified the bodies, you see, and they never doubted us. I mean, after all, if the parents of a young wife say that is their daughter's body, why would anyone think otherwise? Alvin Sechrest's parents were dead, there was only us. It was the easiest thing in the world."

"But, why . . . are you telling me that my mother didn't die then, that my mother is still alive?" An expression of utter astonishment.

Deirdre nodded her head.

"But, why—where?"

"Upstairs. In this house. We made a small apartment up in the tower. In a room in the middle of the tower. That's why I couldn't allow the Garson boy to go up there."

The pretty pink mouth gaped. "In the tower? All these

years?" Deirdre nodded. "But, why? How could she live like that?" A quick jump to a conclusion. "Something is wrong with her. Is that it? Is she insane or something?" Cheryl reached out and dug fingernails into Deirdre's arms. "Tell me."

Deirdre disengaged herself as gently as possible. "No, my dear, she is not insane. She is ill. She's been ill ever since you were born. It happened very quickly, out of the blue. We got you away before there could be any contagion."

"Contagion! What's wrong with her?"

"We've tried everything." Why was it that it was so hard to say the word. "Doctors, at first, of course. The first one diagnosed it and you can imagine how shocked and horrified we were . . . we took her and ran, we knew what they would do with her and we couldn't, wouldn't let that happen to our darling, our beautiful child. Tony and I may not have had much in common, but we had that, an utter and complete love for Leila. We went from place to place, giving false names, seeking treatment but nothing worked, nothing and we didn't dare stay long. So finally we decided that we must look for a place to keep her, where she could live in peace as long as she would live . . ." Her voice broke, she controlled it. "And I don't know how long that will be. You can't imagine the nightmare thoughts I have—what if anything should happen to me or to Tony while she still lives?"

"Grandmother," Cheryl spoke the name quite unconsciously, her expression was intense, her body so tense as to be almost rigid, "what is wrong with my mother?"

"She has . . . Hansen's disease."

No recognition in the clear eyes. She'd have to spell it out. "Leprosy." There, it had been spoken aloud.

"Leprosy." Cheryl whispered the word, fell back in the chaise longue. "But nobody has leprosy . . . it's a disease of the Dark Ages, the Bible."

Deirdre smiled humorlessly. "Believe me, because I've

looked into it, there are millions of cases of leprosy in the world today. Not here in the United States, not so many. It's more common in tropical countries but in certain regions with cooler climates, too, Korea and China, for instance. Here in the United States the chief areas are Texas, California, Hawaii, Louisiana, Florida, and New York."

"But how did she get it? Where did it come from?"

"The causal agent is Hansen's bacillus, mycobacterium leprae. It can be a family infection through close contact and prolonged exposure and we've come to believe that Alvin Sechrest could have had leprosy. We're not certain because we didn't have an autopsy done after the accident, but we did do some investigating into the death of his parents and we've made up our minds that this is where the bacillus could have come from. If his parents had it, you see, and were untreated he could and probably would have developed a mild, single-lesion type of leprosy. Leila could have caught it from him, the incubation period is often three to five years and they were married three years when you were born, she became ill right after."

Cheryl put her hands to her mouth.

"I know you'll want to see her"—Deirdre made her voice matter-of-fact—"but I think it would be better if I prepared you for it. You see, she has the lepromatous form of leprosy. She doesn't feel heat or cold and she has lost her tactile sense. It's a kind of anesthesia caused by the destruction of the peripheral nervous tissue in the affected areas. The lepromatous type of the disease, due to the thickening of the skin, formation of nodules and loss of eyebrows which is characteristic, has given her a leonine facies." Deirdre reached for Cheryl's hand, "I sound like a medical textbook, don't I? My dear, your beautiful mother is no longer beautiful. She has a face like a lion and claw hands. And although she cannot feel pain in the affected areas, she is in severe pain in other parts of her poor, deformed body. At times it is all I can do to keep from throwing myself to the floor and howling when I see her this way."

"No, no," Cheryl mouthed the words.

"One of us is with her at all times, Tony, Florida, Betsy, or myself. And Lindsay when she was here, she was the only outsider who knew. We took shifts, you see, that's why I planned for the nap periods, arranged things so that we would be able to go up to the tower without anyone wondering where we were. It's quite a comfortable room and we give her everything that she can possibly want . . ."

"Why don't you put her in a hospital?" Cheryl wailed.

Deirdre leaned back, took a deep breath. "My dear, you can't possibly know what those places, leprosariums, are like. When I was a little girl I used to summer down this way and there was a leper colony on one of the Elizabeth Islands, the Penikese Island. I heard such tales . . . you wouldn't believe. We couldn't shut her away somewhere, leave her among strangers . . ."

"But you shut her up here!"

"That's different. She is with her family. You can't imagine how she loves and needs me. And we do everything that could possibly be done . . ."

"But there must be new medicines, new treatments, new techniques . . ."

Deirdre nodded. "Oh, yes, they tell you there are. And I used to get very excited, hurry to find out, but when I would ask a doctor or write to a clinic they'd give me some maybe this and if that sort of answer and always end with the stipulation that they had to see a patient before they could treat him. But don't you see, that was the catch. The minute they'd see Leila, they would have taken her away from us. And we couldn't have that, don't you see? So we could never chance it."

Eyes wide, horrified, "And you just leave her up there to die?"

"No, no, she isn't dying. The disease does not have to be fatal . . . we watch her health so very carefully. And she isn't blind yet, so . . ."

"She isn't blind!"

"Well, you see, that does happen sometimes. Except for the pain, and that comes and goes, she is merely disfigured and she does have difficulty with her voice, there's a septal perforation that has caused nasal collapse, it isn't very pretty —my God, what am I saying—it looks terrible, this is what I want to warn you about because she can see and she can understand an expression of horror. If you visit her, I want you to know what to expect. She doesn't know what she looks like because we are very careful to keep mirrors away, oh, she knows about her hands, of course, and she suspects, but she doesn't know. You mustn't let her know how grotesque she has become, she was such a beautiful child and girl, you see . . ."

Cheryl began to weep, a high thin wail that made Deirdre think of banshees.

"Oh, Cheryl, poor child. I'm sorry to have to tell you like this, but once the shock is over you'll feel as we do, willing to do anything to help her. Tony and I have given our lives to keep her safe and happy, as happy as possible. There is nothing I wouldn't do for her—or Tony either, nothing . . ."

The wailing stopped abruptly. "Nothing you wouldn't do for her." Cheryl's voice was wobbly, grew stronger. "Nothing? Evan Garson, you couldn't let him go up into the tower you said . . . What did you do to keep him from going there? Did you do something that caused him to fall? And Chrystal and Forrestor McMann . . . did they find out, was that it? My God, I think I've come to a madhouse!"

Deirdre lost her temper. "Cheryl, don't be a fool. Leila's life is the most important thing in the world to us. We didn't plan to hurt the Garson boy. I told him not to try and climb that ladder. Tony had sawed some high rungs as long as two or three years ago. That was just in case, when I was trying to use outside help to take over the housekeeping so that Florida and Betsy would have more time to spend with Leila. It was simply an accident that Evan Garson climbed the ladder and fell. If he'd listened to me and done as I said, it never would have happened. It was simply a precautionary measure, sawing those rungs. And as for Chrystal, she was a greedy, scheming immoral woman and if she'd been a true friend rather than a calculating witch she'd still be alive today. And Forrestor, well Forrestor truly did have a bad heart and he did have a heart attack because he was someplace he shouldn't be, he went up the stairs to the tower and he shouldn't have done that, he was in the wrong place and he knew it. I cannot control people, I cannot be blamed, either, for the situations they get themselves into."

"The stairs to the tower? Then there are other stairs, of course, there must be." Cheryl's eyes were dry now, her face had lost its completely disbelieving look.

"Yes, behind my bedroom is a passageway. When we bought the house, we had workmen come from New York and fix things. They wouldn't be around, you see, to gossip at the local bar. I should have had the front ladder removed at that time, that's what I should have done, but we thought it would look strange to anyone who'd been in the place previously, might make them suspicious, you know, like a delivery man or some such. And we couldn't lock the door for the same reasons, it was the quickest way to the other wing. Although Florida did lock her side at night." She smiled wryly. "She could shut danger out. I didn't dare."

Cheryl straightened. "Let me get this right. Just to be sure I haven't misunderstood. You have my mother who is not dead but is suffering from leprosy living up in the tower. You —or Tony, rather—booby-trapped the ladder so that anyone trying to get up to the tower would fall and break his neck, and somebody did. Chrystal found out about something—

my mother or the ladder, no probably the ladder because I think you could have coerced her into accepting the other, so you—or Tony, yes, certainly Tony—fixed the brakes on the car, and then Forrestor McMann died of a heart attack because he found the way up to the tower. This is what I think you told me just now, sitting there and looking as though you were talking about the celery crop or the lobster shortage."

Deirdre relaxed. The girl did have the Dunn character, after all. If she could speak so coolly, she'd come to accept and help. No tie stronger than that of blood. "I haven't told Leila you are here," she said. "I'll want to tell her before you see her. It will be quite a shock to her, as well. She didn't ever expect to see you again."

"What did you tell her? That I was dead, too?" Yes, there was sarcasm in the voice, but that was all right. Color had returned to Cheryl's face and stiffness to her spine.

"No, she knows you were with Alice. Alice was Leila's friend as well as mine, closer in age to your mother than to me, actually. But she'll be so pleased to see her child again after all these years. I know she will, even if she may not show it. The face, you see—well, never mind that now. I'll tell her you're coming and when you're ready, we'll go. But, Cheryl, give yourself some time to prepare yourself. As I said before, I don't want her to see you react in the wrong way."

Cheryl didn't answer, stared into space. As good a time as any, thought Deirdre, for me to see Leila. She'll have been fed by Florida, be expecting me anyway. She brushed crumbs off her skirt and rose.

"You didn't mention the two drownings the police chief spoke of." Cheryl sounded laconic. "A gardener and a maid, wasn't it? Were they helped along the way by you—or Tony?"

Deirdre thought quickly that Cheryl had heard all that she needed to know. "Of course not," she said serenely. "When shall I tell Leila you'll be coming?"

"I—don't know—yet. You've told me so many things . . .

given me so much to take in . . ." They exchanged glances, the girl's eyes were wet. "Please—give me some time."

"I understand." Deirdre patted Cheryl's shoulder and left her sitting on the porch. She found Tony waiting in the gym.

"Well," he asked, "how did she take it?"

"She's sitting out there—crying, I think."

"What are you going to do now?"

"Wait."

"Wait for what?"

"To see if she's strong enough."

"And if she isn't?"

"She's got to be. She's our granddaughter."

"She looks more like her father than her mother. I think she does, I don't really remember. Maybe that's why—I don't know why I don't trust her."

"That's because she's a lot like me."

"God help us," said Tony sincerely.

Deirdre, coming down from the tower, allowed herself the luxury of tears. Leila was having a bad day, there was a lot of pain. Tony would have to drive into Boston and get some more morphine, the supply was dwindling. Deirdre had managed to steal a pad of prescription blanks from Dr. Chesney a few years back when she'd gone to him complaining of arthritis. Onto these, laboriously at first, but now easily she copied an original prescription for morphine and forged Dr. Chesney's name. In a big city drugstore, it was never questioned.

She stopped at her bathroom and washed her face. The house was silent, lifeless. She'd miss the silly antics of the Hinkle boys, how they could make her laugh; Clive's tacit adoration. Poor Clive, longing to be like other men but by instinct a homosexual. Yes, he adored her with a chaste adoration, no demands on her person. It was so very pleasant.

153

But she'd have to do without any of it. Already she missed them all. How nice it had been to have something, someone to look forward to at the end of each distressing day.

Tony was coming up the stairs as she was coming down. He was hurrying and she asked quickly, "What's the matter?"

"The girl said she was going down to the beach."

"So?"

"She took her pocketbook and no swim suit."

"That doesn't necessarily mean anything."

"Yes, it does. She isn't down there. I just looked. She isn't anywhere."

"How long ago did she leave?"

"Fifteen-twenty minutes. Something like that. Maybe thirty."

"And you're sure she's not in the house or on the grounds?"

"Certain."

She set her teeth. "What did you say to her?"

"Nothing." Spoken without expression. Sometimes she wondered if he felt anything any more. Even fear.

"Of course you did. You threatened her. I should keep you on a leash." She'd set the girl up, Tony, stupidly, obviously had set her off. There were times when she could kill him, literally squash him like a huge, repulsive insect. But she needed him. Damn it, she needed him. Completely frustrated, she struck out at him.

He grabbed her arm, easily fended her off. "All I told her was, don't get any smart ideas. People who get smart ideas do dumb things. If they're not careful, they get hurt. Words to the wise, I told her. I was playing the grampa, giving grandfatherly advice."

Deirdre took a deep breath, she'd deal with him later. She asked herself, "Where could she have gone?"

"You're the smart one. How am I supposed to figure out what's on her mind?"

"I wonder if she could have . . . no, it can't be to the police. She's flesh and blood, she wouldn't. Unless you used a heavy hand . . ."

Tony didn't answer, only stared. His eyes looked so blank, she thought fleetingly of a hollowed-out log. "I'll drive into town," she decided aloud. "Maybe I'll find her walking. In case I don't—you'd better make sure that everything's in order upstairs. Thank God, she's sleeping. I just gave her a shot. It seems to be getting worse again, it just breaks my heart . . ." She stopped, no time now. "Go on. Do as I told you. Upstairs."

"That's just where I was going."

They passed each other, going opposite directions.

I underestimated her, thought Deirdre. That was very foolish of me to underestimate the girl. And yet, the alternatives are there, I've taken precautions, always knew, feared that someone one day would tell . . . She hurried now, and realized she was elated. A new challenge. Deirdre Dunn had always thrived on a new challenge. A new part in a new play written by a new and inexperienced author.

Megagerma Lyra, *the Asiatic false vampire is relatively large, carnivorous. They hunt along walls, tree trunks and vegetation, moving slowly and deliberately up and down with a hovering sort of flight.*

Chief Griffin . . .

I'm sixty-three years old, he thought, and I've never been to California or had a beautiful woman kiss me or won as much as a nickel in any kind of contest. George Griffin laced his hands over a small but burgeoning paunch and felt sorry for himself.

The electric fan tried its best to cheer him, but it was a poor little fan, not big enough nor new enough and anyway anybody else worth a hill of beans had air conditioning in his office.

But did he deserve any better? He considered that. He wasn't a very good cop, he tried but he just didn't have the knack for it. Nor the experience. All his adult life spent in Truro. So there were housebreaks and now and again somebody knocked off a supermarket or a coin-operated laundry. And the bloody, messy accidents. And the family fights. Now and again a drowning. How was a man to get onto any tricks of the trade if he didn't find a body maybe packed into a trunk or some big-shot mobster didn't try to take over the town and fill it with gambling parlors and cathouses?

He took a cigar from his desk, lit it and puffed on it for comfort. It didn't taste very good. Couldn't be the cigar, must be George Griffin. What was eating at him anyhow? All the goings-on at Belfry House. The old boy who took his shiny musical saw and fixed a car so it would smack into a tree. Sounded all right for the television, maybe, but here, in Truro, it left a bad taste in his mouth. The way he looked at it, people didn't do things just like that. Leastwise, the people he'd known didn't. 'Course that bunch at Belfry House—they were different, all right. Another world. So how could he tell? For sure?

He liked to know things for sure, that was the way he was. He would have liked to pick up all those ladder bits and piece that ladder back together if there'd been any sense to it. Only, once he got it back the way it was—which he couldn't do because some of it was splintered and it looked to him like they'd missed some pieces, too, or maybe they were still hanging at the top—how could it make anything plain to him? Like, could it tell if anybody pushed the Garson boy off the ladder? Fingerprints? Well, maybe. The books and the TV and the movies made a big thing of fingerprints, but it had been his experience that often they were all smeared and you couldn't get a good print and if you did you had a hell of a time finding the man whose print matched up with it. Especially with a force the size of his.

The electric fan blew warm air into his face. Another scorcher of a day, more than half over now and what did he have to look forward to when the sun went down? Fish cakes and beans, leftovers at that and he didn't care much for them when they were brand new; and nothing but reruns on the black and white television and color TV was still sky high in price even though they'd said years ago that mass production would bring the cost down.

160

He put his cigar in an ashtray that had *The World's Worst Bowler*—that was his wife's idea of a joke—written on it, and let the cigar burn itself out. One thing about cigars, you could always light them up again even though sometimes they tasted terrible. It just wasn't the way it should be. Everybody should make some kind of killing at least once in his lifetime.

There was a quick rap on his door and Abner Kitchener, without waiting even for so much as a come in, looked in at him. "Somebody wants to see you, Chief. I found her picking them up and putting them down on Route 3."

Chief Griffin took his feet off his desk, barely had time to do that, when Cheryl Harris came into his office and sat, like she was ready to drop, in a chair.

She looked awful, for her. Her face was red from the heat and drops of sweat stood out on her upper lip. Her long blonde hair was tangled as though she'd combed it with an egg beater and her blue dress was dark at the waist with perspiration.

Abner stood in the doorway and beamed like he'd brought home the prize package. "Get the little lady a cup of water," the chief told him, "and then get back on duty." This just wasn't the day Abner was going to get any handclaps from yours truly, he thought.

"Now you just rest a minute," he told the girl. "You look like you've had a time of it."

"I didn't realize it was such a long way." She found a tissue in her pocketbook, wiped her face with it.

"You walked all the way from Belfry House?" The chief shook his head.

Abner came in with the water and she thanked him before downing it thirstily. Then she nodded in reply to the chief's question.

"Nobody gave you a ride?" How comes, he wondered, they didn't bring her in?

"I didn't think I needed one. Strangers, I didn't think I

wanted to ride with strangers . . . I was afraid they'd find I'd gone and come after me. For the longest time, I stayed off the road so they wouldn't see me if they came looking."

Abner stood there gawking and looking foolish and the chief sent him on his way. "They? Who's they? And why didn't Miss Dunn give you the use of the other car? They've got a station wagon besides that Pinto, haven't they?"

"They? Deirdre, I mean, Miss Dunn. She and Tony Nero. That's who I mean when I say they." She leaned forward earnestly and the fan's breeze stirred her hair. "I didn't know what to do and I thought about it and thought about it, trying to tell myself I had to go along with them but all the time I knew it was wrong, dreadfully wrong, so I came to tell you. I'll go back out there with you to show you, I've made up my mind to do that even though I don't want to, even though I'm so very frightened, I can't bear the thought of looking at her . . ."

"Who? Miss Dunn?"

She shook her head, hair flew and her face crumpled. Griffin thought she was going to cry, but she didn't. Still, her voice wobbled when she said, "No, not Miss Dunn. Her daughter. My mother. I'm Deirdre Dunn's granddaughter and she's got my mother shut up in the tower of Belfry House. You've got to get her out of there, send her to a hospital! They're killing her just as they killed Chrystal and Forrestor McMann and Evan Garson, too, I think they did that, too, and maybe others, maybe those two who drowned . . ."

Two years away from retirement and this has to happen, thought Chief Griffin bitterly. "Now, hold on a minute, Miss Harris. Slow down. You're all heated up, take it easy. One thing at a time. You're Miss Dunn's granddaughter? How comes nobody said you're her granddaughter? I don't recall anybody saying anything about you being related. Miss Dunn told me you were the child of a friend who died a short time back. So, how could you be her granddaughter?" There was

162

a fancy New York psychiatrist who summered out on the other side of town, Griffin wondered if he was out at his summer place. He didn't think Doc Chesney could handle this one.

The girl made an effort to pull herself together. Give her credit, she did lower her voice and began to speak more slowly. "Deirdre left me with Alice Harris when I was a baby. Because of my mother, but I didn't know that. Not until today. I just thought Deirdre didn't want me around so I came here to tell her what I thought of her, face to face. I did that, but I didn't tell the others who I was and she didn't either. Too ashamed, I guess. Too many explanations. Only, I did tell Forrestor that day on the beach . . ."

She was off again, words coming faster, voice getting louder and higher in tone. "Okay, okay, you say you're Miss Dunn's granddaughter. But the way I understand it, your mother died a long time ago. And now you tell me she lives in the tower at Belfry House?" His doubt showed, he knew, but Lord Almighty, how could he hide it?

She nodded vehemently. "She didn't die, you see. That was all a lie. It was some other woman in the car with my father and my mother has this terrible disease, Deirdre wanted to take me up to see her, but I don't want to see her, can you understand that? I mean, it sounds, so ghastly, leprosy, even the word terrifies me. But she's got to get out of there and get the proper treatment. They're out of their minds, all of them, Deirdre and Tony and Florida and Betsy. All conspiring in this fantastic pretense. I sat and listened to Deirdre tell me all this and I thought I was going mad myself. It's a nightmare, a nightmare!"

Leprosy? Had she said leprosy? She had. When he was a boy, he'd been out in a boat near Penikese Island and somebody had said there were lepers there and after that he never went near the place again. Even after they cleared the island out, never could tell what kind of germs hung in the very air. He realized he had suddenly developed a very bad headache, one minute he was just tired and mixed-up and the next he had this headache.

"Chrystal found out something, you see." The girl spoke more easily now, as though she'd gotten past the worst part. "So they had to get rid of Chrystal and they blamed it on Forrestor McMann so they had to get rid of him, too!"

"You mean to tell me that all those people lived in that house and all this was going on and nobody knew nothing?"

"Lindsay Ball knows, Deirdre told me that. If you don't believe me, you can ask Lindsay Ball. Only, she's gone to her sister's—I don't know where her sister lives. You can make Deirdre tell you and you can get in touch with Lindsay . . ."

Play along with her, that was the thing to do. And when she'd calmed down, call the Harding fella in the Attorney General's office, maybe he'd know what to do. She was going on, saying, "And the cook and the maid, they know. I don't know how she's kept them quiet, money, maybe, but you can force them to tell you, can't you?"

"Well, I guess we can talk to them, Miss Harris, but in the meantime, what's going to happen to you? You look mighty upset to me and I reckon from what you say you don't want to stay back at Belfry House. Did you leave your things there? Want me to go out and get them, we'll see if we can't get you a room at one of the motels if they're not all filled up, or a guest house, we'll find a place for you somewhere."

She looked taken aback. "I never thought—I suppose I can't just go home?"

He surely wished she could. Just go away and forget the whole thing. But she'd sat there and made all those wild accusations and even if they sounded like a crock full of nuts, he had to look into it. Something awful funny out at Belfry House, no matter how you studied it. "I'd say you'll have to stay around until we get this straightened out." He reached up and rubbed his temples, throbbing, they were.

She set her mouth hard. "In that case, let's go right out there. I'll tell her what I told you, right to her face, and she'll have to let you go up to the tower, she will, won't she? I mean, can't you get a search warrant or something?"

How in blazes would he get up in that tower? He had no intention of putting his weight on that rickety ladder. "The ladder that goes up there is busted," he reminded her.

"There's a stairway in Deirdre's room. Like a back stairway. She told me where it was. I'll show you."

Chief Griffin inhaled deeply, got up and went to the door. He opened it and called out to Abner who was on the desk, "Get Tinkham to come in and tend the office, I don't care if it is his day off. And dig out a search warrant, we may need it." He left the door open, came back to his chair and wished he knew exactly what to do next. Go to Belfry House, there was no way out of that. But what to do when he got there if he found what the girl said he'd find. He got up again, went back to the door and added, "And get Doc Chesney, see if you can round him up, too."

When he sat down again, the girl's eyes were not so wild, but bright just the same, and she said, "I know all this sounds crazy, but you'll see when we get there. You'll see."

The lights were on at Belfry House even though it wasn't dark yet, just turning dusk. It looked so peaceful sitting there all by itself, a strange old house, too big for anybody to live in. The tower loomed dark against a purpling sky. Birds flew around it, they looked like birds.

Kitchener was driving, he braked at the side of the porch steps but nobody got out right away. The chief sighed, rubbed his head, opened the door on his side. Dr. Chesney and Miss Harris were in the back seat, Doc Chesney made the first move there and then they all got out, stood on the steps.

Footsteps sounded inside, in the hall. A figure dressed in

white came to the door, looked out, said, "Thank God. Where did you find her?" It was Deirdre Dunn.

"I found them," said Cheryl Harris a little too loudly. "I told them, Deirdre. Now I've come to show them."

Deirdre opened the screen door. "Come in. I've been so worried."

Everybody waited for everyone else to climb the steps. Then, shoulders back, the girl went ahead and the others followed. Tony Nero stood halfway down the hall, waiting. "Is she all right?" he asked.

"Yes, I'm all right now." Cheryl's tone was high and clear. She turned left to the stairway. "We're going up to the tower. I've brought the police to see what's in the tower."

"Oh, Cheryl." Deirdre sounded miserably unhappy. "My dear. You really don't want to go up there, do you?"

"Oh, yes." Standing on the third step, the girl turned and looked back at the older woman. "Yes, indeed. We certainly do. You can't stop us."

Deirdre made a gesture of resignation. "I have no intention of stopping anybody. Go, if you must. It won't be very pleasant, but I suppose we must face the truth."

Cheryl smiled, not a pretty smile. "Aren't you coming with us?"

"No."

"You'd better leave somebody down here, Chief Griffin." The girl sounded frightened again. He signaled Abner to stay.

Deirdre smiled this time, an ironic smile. "We'll wait in the drawing room. Tony," she called over her shoulder, "shouldn't you get them some flashlights?"

"We won't need them," the girl answered quickly, but, Griffin thought, a little uncertainly. "There's electricity up there. There has to be."

"Well, yes, I think there is—or there was at one time, but I'm not sure it's working or whether there are any bulbs. It's been so long since anyone's been up there." Deirdre looked flustered.

Cheryl laughed. The chief didn't like the sound of it.

"Here, take these just in case." Tony Nero brought flashlights, handed them to the chief and to the doctor.

The chief tested his. It worked. He looked up at the girl. She turned slowly and started up the stairs, began to move more quickly as she climbed, almost ran.

She chose a door on the third floor, opened it on a blue and green and white room, went directly to hanging green draperies at the back of a big bed and pushed the draperies aside to reveal a door. She reached out for the knob, hesitated, turned it. They could make out steps going up to darkness. The steps looked dusty where Chief Griffin flashed his light. He found a switch at the bottom of the stairs, but when he pushed it, nothing happened.

"I'll lead the way," he said. "Doc, you bring up the rear."

The staircase was narrow. They made their way, single file, the girl stumbled once and the chief reached back to steady her. At the top was another door. An old door of brown varnished wood. The light shone on its black glass doorknob.

They listened. Rustling sounds—outside? Night sounds? Griffin could hear himself, the others breathing hard.

"Well, open it," said Cheryl. Her voice was tight.

He turned the knob. The door creaked as it opened. He played his light inside, along the walls, stepped back involuntarily. Cheryl, looking in behind him, gave a single shrill scream that split the darkness.

Dr. Chesney added his light. Bats. Looked like hundreds of them. Hanging upside down from the walls, the ceiling. They stirred in the light, moved their wings, emitted little squeaks. One came from the ceiling, began to soar closer and closer; then came another and another.

"Shut the door!" the girl cried.

"Move," Griffin told Doc Chesney who stood, bemused, between the girl and the steps down.

"Never in my life saw so many bats," said the doctor almost to himself. He turned, much too slowly to suit the chief, and began his retreat. They came after him, forced to his pace. For God's sake, the chief was thinking, get the hell out of here. Can't stand them. If there's one thing that gives me chills, it's bats!

Back in the fancy bedroom, the girl said, voice wobbling, "They've hidden her."

The two men looked at each other. "Let's go downstairs and talk," suggested Griffin.

"Yes. We'll find her. If they won't tell us, we'll find her ourselves. We'll go through every room." And she ran out into the hall, began opening doors, slamming them shut in disappointment.

The men walked silently by her, heard her follow. They marched down the stairs, tramped into the gold and white living room. Deirdre and Tony sat waiting, Tony had something in his hand that he put into his pocket. It looked like a book of matches. The cook and the maid were there, too, faces expressionless.

"I'm sorry," said Deirdre Dunn. "The bats don't bother anyone, but most people are afraid of them." She looked to Dr. Chesney. "What do we do now? We want to help in anyway we can."

"What did you do with her?" demanded Cheryl. "What did you do with my mother?"

Deirdre stood up and went to her. "Oh, my poor child." She reached out but the girl moved away. "She's ill," Deirdre told them sadly. "I've seen it coming on and then today when she accused us of all these unbelievable things, I knew we would have to get treatment for her. I put in a call to your office, Doctor, but you were out and then we discovered she'd run away. I'm afraid her foster mother's death started it all, she and Alice were so close."

"Then she is your granddaughter?" asked Griffin.

"Oh, yes. I take some of the blame for this. I should have kept her with me or, at least, told her that Alice was not her real mother. She found that out only after Alice's death and that shock right after the other . . ." Her dark eyes grew damp. "And, then of course, the awfulness of what happened here."

The girl's blue eyes blazed fire and her face contorted. "No, no, you don't," she shouted, voice ragged, "you're lying!" She turned to Griffin, clutched at his arm. "Make her tell you where she's hidden my mother. She's somewhere in this house, she's got to be, she's ill. They couldn't have taken her anywhere else! Look for her, damn you! Look! I'm not insane. She's here, I tell you!"

"You may search, of course." Deirdre's face became a mask of sorrow. "But Florida and Betsy here, they'd have no reason to lie, they'll tell you there's no one in this house except us."

"They'd lie! Of course they'd lie. They've lied for years, she pays them to lie." The girl, in a fury, clenched her fists and began to strike Deirdre Dunn. Kitchener grabbed her from behind, wound his arms around her. She thrashed, then subsided, sobbing.

"I'd say a sedative and a little rest would be the thing right now." Dr. Chesney set his black bag on a table and opened it, ready for business.

"Yes, we'll put her to bed." Deirdre's velvet voice throbbed with sympathy.

"Not here! I won't stay here!" She struggled in Kitchener's grasp. "Look for my mother." The last was a wail, almost a howl.

"All right, all right." The chief motioned to Abner to take her. "You go out and sit in the car, Miss Harris. The doctor will go along and give you something to make you feel better. We'll look around here and then we'll take you into town where the doc here can take care of you. Be a good girl so we can get on with it."

"You're lying to me, too." How a pretty girl could look so ugly was a strange thing to Griffin. "They lie and now you lie. You won't look because you don't believe me."

"We'll look," he said patiently.

"Come on, Miss Harris." Abner nudged her toward the door.

Her eyes grew dull and all the fire went out. "I don't know how they did it. But they had time. Take her out, move the furniture, let the bats come in, throw dirt on the stairs . . ." And then, as though realizing what she had said, she whispered, bewildered, "How did they do it?"

When Abner and Dr. Chesney had taken her out, Deirdre shaded her eyes with her hand and said, "And now, if you wish, the house is yours. We'll show you anything you wish to see."

He'd promised and because he'd promised, he started to go with the women. "I'm real sorry about this," he said.

"Will she have to be shut up? In a sanitarium?" Tony Nero wanted to know.

"We'll take care of any costs," Deirdre assured him. "I'm certain it's just a temporary thing. I hope so. I want her to be with us. Where she belongs."

The chief didn't know the answer so he didn't answer. He followed the servants, had them open doors, closet doors, cupboard doors, it was a very large house and it took quite some time. And all the while he knew he wouldn't find anything.

He didn't. And that called for more apologies all around which took more time, but he didn't mind that so much because he dreaded telling the girl.

She took it better than he expected, but then the doc had

given her something. "I know. I know, they planned it too well. Just let me go home, please. I'll be all right."

"We'll see, we'll see," said Dr. Chesney soothingly. It was said in Truro that Dr. Chesney had a very nice bedside manner.

The Phinopomatidae, *the most primitive living family of Microchiroptera, the mouse-tailed bats are thought to have competed poorly in nature and have thus been passed by evolutionarily. In Egypt, they often roost in tombs and are sometimes called tomb bats.*

Tony Nero . . .

He didn't sleep the night through, he hadn't for years, matter of fact he couldn't remember when he last had. Too much on his mind. Too much —and yet really only one thing nowadays and that one thing was too much. Why didn't he care what happened to anybody? Why?

How had that come about? When he was young, he'd been like everybody else. Full of hope and the milk of human kindness.

It was Deirdre's fault. Never respecting him. Saying she loved him, marrying him, then using him for whatever she wanted. He was all burned out inside from being used.

The only pleasure he got any more was being awake in the night and playing with matches.

The orange and yellow flame (touched with blue) in the night was a beautiful thing. He could see pretty pictures in short-lived fires.

Sometimes in the night he'd go through three or four packs of matches, lighting them and letting them burn as long as they would, stopping just short of burning his fingers. And picking up the burned matches, mustn't let Deirdre find them. She had told him to *STOP THAT* but he hadn't. The one thing she'd told him to do that he'd paid no attention to. Ha-ha.

Sometimes he thought how nice a big fire would be. Not a fireplace fire, although those were nice, too, but a real big fire. When he thought those thoughts, he'd put some papers in a metal waste basket and take it outside, away from the house where Deirdre couldn't see, and set them ablaze.

He made himself do that because he knew what kind of fire he really wanted to see.

Belfry House going up in flames.

Little orange and yellow (touched with blue) tongues flickering at all the windows.

The only thing that kept his fingers from holding a lighted match to the gold drapes in the living room was the fact that if he did it, he'd have nothing to look forward to. Everybody needed something to look forward to.

His watch had a luminous dial. He looked at it now . . . 4:05 A.M. Everybody sleeping. Deirdre. Florida. Betsy. Leila.

Leila. Better off dead.

He lit a match.

The girl had made a big stink, he knew Deirdre shouldn't have told her.

The girl was some kind of witch, sent by somebody, maybe God, to punish him for the awful things Deirdre had made him do. God thought he hadn't had enough punishment. Well, God was wrong!

The girl took after Deirdre.

But she had a right to—she was Deirdre's granddaughter. And his, too. Deirdre shouldn't have talked to the police that way, made them think the girl was off her rocker. What would happen to the girl? Would they put her away some-where? Like they'd put Leila away? Deirdre would rather die than let them put Leila away. How comes she didn't feel the same about Leila's daughter? 'Cause she'd hated the man that took Leila away and married her? Who could under-stand Deirdre? He'd never been able to.

The bat scene had worked well. Deirdre'd said it would. There'd been a few bats at Belfry House in the beginning and Deirdre had sent for more ("Making a moving picture") and they'd made a real bat house out of that tower room. Behind it was Leila's room. Nobody would look for another room behind a wall of bats.

'Course they had to go through them every time they went in or out. But he didn't mind them. Didn't like them either. Nasty-looking things. But they didn't hurt anybody. Not like some people he knew.

He lit a match.

He didn't care personally if the cops found out except that maybe they'd put him away and if that happened, he'd be better off dead.

Serve Deirdre right.

Do this, Tony, do that, Tony . . . don't you think it would be better if . . . you must do this, Tony, if you don't . . .

He wanted to hate Deirdre but he didn't hate her, not if hate was supposed to be a burning anger. Full of fire and fury. Ouch, the match licked at his fingers. He dropped it. No, he didn't hate her. He just dreamed of doing something that would fix her wagon. But good.

But she had the money.

He could have told the chief today about Leila, that would have been a good wagon-fixer.

But then Deirdre would tell them things back. About the drowning, not the gardener, he'd had nothing to do with that, just copied it, but it was that stupid little female's fault, spying around, finding the door behind Deirdre's bed. Deirdre said they must get rid of her and so he'd copied the way the gardener died. Should have stuck to it, too, but Deirdre said no. Too suspicious. Deirdre had the brains and the money.

And the rungs on the ladder. "Wouldn't it be wise to make sure no one climbs the front stairs? If you sawed some of the rungs up high where they wouldn't be noticed, no one could get up. Oh, I know we could keep that way into the tower locked but nonetheless, someone might get curious and go up and hear something . . ." So he had and Evan Garson had gotten curious two years later and had fallen and was that his fault?

He lit a match.

Pure coincidence that he'd used McMann's saw on the Pinto, but it worked out okay. His house saw was rusted, left it out in the rain, somebody did, and Forrestor's was nice and shiny, handy, very handy. Still, if Chrystal had driven more carefully would she be better off dead now?

As for McMann's heart attack, he'd put the strong arm on the old man because Deirdre found him in the tower and said . . . no matter. He hadn't killed Forrestor; Forrestor had obliged because of his weak heart.

And wasn't there another—a long, long time ago—yes, the one in the beginning, the car and the man and the woman, such a long time ago that he had almost forgotten, wasn't even sure he'd done it.

So let her tell them. He didn't care.

Yes, he did! Hey, that was great. There was something that he cared about. Rather than be shut up someplace, he'd be better off dead. He cared about something.

Only—wasn't he shut up here?

He lit two matches and held them up to each side of his head and looked at himself in the dark mirror. Ronald the Robot, that had been his name on the TV, looked back at him.

That's what he was. A robot. Not caring. Taking commands.

"Tony! What are you doing?"

Deirdre's face appeared behind his in the mirror, like a ghost's.

"Nothing." He shook the matches out.

"Well, go to bed. And stop fooling around with those matches. You know this place could go up like a tinderbox, I've told you a thousand times. I swear, sometimes I think you're retarded."

He could still imagine the faces in the glass, only now, without the matches, they were pale burs on black. "Did you ever love me, Deirdre?"

"What a ridiculous question! Will you go to bed?"

"I loved you, Deirdre. I was crazy about you."

"You were just plain crazy. Will you do what I say!" She moved closer and although he couldn't see it clearly, he knew the kind of expression that was on her face. It was the look that made him do things. He wasn't sure why that look made him do things he didn't want to do. He hated that look. Yes, hated! He felt the sudden fury. What a great feeling.

"Someday, Deirdre, I'll get back at you."

A sharp silence while she thought about that. Then she laughed. "You'll never have the nerve. I'm your nerve, Tony, and you know it. If I want you to act, you act. If I say no, you don't."

"Say no, Deirdre." He imagined that her eyes darkened in the silver black of the mirror.

She laughed again, such a sure laugh. "No. Now, go to bed."

He laughed, too, then, and turned and placed his big hands around her throat. He hadn't planned it, how nice her neck felt, how soft, how squeezable. She fought him, but it was nothing. There was a television commercial—don't squeeze the—neck! He squeezed and squeezed.

And, when she lay quietly, he lit a match and held it out to the gold drapes.